Power Riches Or Death -PROD
Vol. II
THE DIAMOND KING

POWER RICHES
OR DEATH - PROD
VOL. II

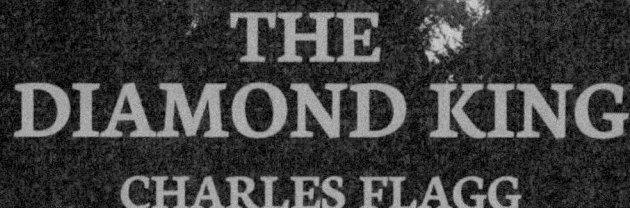

THE
DIAMOND KING
CHARLES FLAGG

Power Riches Or Death -PROD Vol. II, THE DIAMOND KING
© 2025, by Charles Flagg

ISBN: 979-8-9923201-0-7

Published by Regal Rhythms Poetry LLC
Printed in the United States of America

Edited by: Regal Rhythms Poetry LLC
Cover Art: Adam Hayden

ACKNOWLEDGEMENTS

I thank everyone who supported me throughout this life changing dream making process.

CONTENTS

Chapter 1

After I rinsed the blood and defeat off me, my soul felt cleansed. Renewed. No regrets and no turning back. It is what the fuck it is. All black was perfect for tonight's occasion. I will visit the Bishop. Either he has the money, or I will baptize him by fire in front of his congregation. Turtle snaked me out of the multi-unit commercial contract. His only available option was to sign it over to me. Negotiations are over with. Find Stormy...get the $1,000,000.00 that she stole from me while suckin' and fuckin' that young nigga.... My partial to-do list was complete. My truck was fresh out of the shop with a new triple coat matte finish and Limo tint windows. I removed the license plate and disconnected the GPS to add another layer to my stealthiness. Low-key tonight, ghost guns, clean bullets, black mask, gorilla tape, zip ties and several pairs of black nitrile gloves. The inventory for the murder bag was complete. I had a burner cell phone for limited communication, and to set the trap for these conniving backstabbers.

"Bishop," I said over the phone, "It seems we have a problem. Checks are bouncing and my money is missing." I was posted outside of his church just in case he tried to make a run for it. That Rolls Royce freshly detailed all pretty and shiny might be exactly where they find him slumped and incapacitated.

Bishop spoke like he was giving a sermon, "Money missing? Brother Craft, now you know our arrangements stem from them gambling markers that you paid for me. I'm in no position to even risk it all by being so foolish."

"I also have them photos of your indiscretions in case you try to get cute. Those young ladies that you enjoy so well," I quickly reminded the snake oil salesman.

"I'm a sinner saved by grace, for God gave his only…"

Interrupting his narcissistic dialogue, "Shut the fuck up, where is my money, Bishop?"

Bishop continued to deny his culpability, "I'm not in charge of the distribution. I delegated those responsibilities to Sister Evans. You know she has an accounting degree. She is real good with numbers. Plus, her son...... you know the boy who works at the REC."

"Pace?" I said in complete disbelief.

"Yeah, Antonio. Yeah, that's him. They have been working on that. I had no idea that was going on, Brother Craft, I promise."

I punched my steering wheel like a heavy bag to relieve some stress. "Your promises don't mean shit. I know where I can find Pace. Where is Sister Evans? It seems these bitches all got sticky fingers."

He hesitated before revealing her location, "Sister Evans is uh, well brother, she is in my office helping with paperwork."

"Well, I guess it's time for a meeting, Bishop, don't you think?" The question was rhetorical. I was already halfway to meet the chief deceiver before I disconnected the call. I walked into this massive building called the Lord's Cathedral, it is one of my best investments and shelters for my cash. All of the thangs' people enjoy seeing: angels and miracles. This man has an anointing I tell you. He is a man that God put me on this earth to bring hell to. Balding, round and out of shape, but an eloquent bullshitter. He participates in the same invitation only parties I attend.

Large mansions with several floors and rooms where people indulge or overindulge in drugs, alcohol, sex, you name it, is there. No cell phones, purses or pockets allowed. Just an appetite for lust and discretion, maybe even perversion is a qualification for the club as well. Sister Evans is thick and mild mannered with a small waistline and natural big booty. Her glitzy hat slanted like a crown giving off an aura of crookedness. The kind that I liked to watch stand up as I sit in the back row at church as an adolescent. Her skin milk chocolate and clear with familiar features. Her smile is disarming, if you didn't know any better. Her hands small with a French tip manicure and crystals on each pinky nail. She confidently extended her daintily hand so I could shake it. I extended mine to crush hers. She began shouting and grimacing. Without speaking, my eyes commanded her silence. Sister Evans dropped to her knees from out of the black, executive leather throne opposite of Bishop.

"Where is my fucking money? Before you lie, I'm not going to ask you again? Don't look at him, look at me," I compressed her hand even tighter as my commands reached her ears. "Bishop can't help you. I own him! I won him in a poker game. God himself put me here to keep guys like him in check," I said, accepting my calling from above.

Pathetically, she put her one finger up as if to motion me to time out. I ignored her sign language and continued to correct her wrongdoing. "In certain places in the world they cut off the hand of thieves and you are definitely a thief," I reminded her. Filled with rage while enjoying every bit of this interrogation, I snatched the letter opener from the Bishop's desk and pierced her directly in the palm of her thieving hand. "My money better be back in my accounts tonight," I spoke, looking her directly in her remorseless eyes. "Bishop, I'm confiscating that new Rolls Royce. You be having bitches all in the stars in the back of it, huh. Tomorrow don't take up no tithes, you greedy bastard. Tell the folk God put it on your heart to have a give back Sunday," I ordered him.

"Umm, umm," he muttered in shock. Like I was the only one who had to pay fines for the failures of my soldiers.

"I ain't asking, Bish-op. I'm telling you." I turned my eyes back to peek into the soul of the thief kneeling before me. "Sister Evans, now I gots' to go visit that son of yours. He at a club trying to turn up with my money. It seems his friend has allowed him to think that my money is for everybody to fuck on and fuck off. That's my bad for misrepresenting myself. I accept all responsibility for my part in all of this," I said with slow and deliberate pauses speaking directly to the souls of my extortioners. "Everyone has their

5

orders......... and I have your addresses. You might want to talk to the Bishop if you think calling the police is an option."

The Bishop sat in his chair shaking his head in disbelief and agreement. "Sister Evans, call yo' son and tell him I'm on my way. If he doesn't come looking for me, for harming his mother, then you know the type of coward you raised." I left with no sense of urgency. I ignored the gawkers staring and whispering while I walked out vindicated and calm. I know what I did was necessary, right or wrong ain't even in the equation.

On my way into the darkest of night, I tried to find a Diamond King and a momma's boy, named Pace. My phone rang. It was Angie and tonight is gonna' be the night.

"Hey beautiful. How you doin'?" I said, in my bedroom voice.

"It's messed up what you did to Stormy," she said with all type of attitude.

"What is it you think I did?" I questioned already knowing the answer.

"I heard that you choked her. Did you?" Angie asked being nosey as usual. Her mouth watered for the tea.

"Who lied to you about me and mines?" I said, pretending to be offended.

"Turtle told me. You know he gossips like a female sometimes. He is very fond of Stormy; I know you know that, but anywayz. Yeah, he told me, so I'm verifying if it is true or not," she wanted to know.

"She was corrected for doing something that she wasn't authorized to do. It seems Turtle should focus on being more of a man to his woman, and not focus so much on what used to belong to me. But I will get up with him and have a lil chat," I spoke in a tone knowing his days were numbered.

"Don't put me in it. I was just wondering cause', it sounds out of your character."

"My character evolves depending on the situation. On another note, be available when I call," I said, changing the subject abruptly.

"What time you coming? I was going out to the club to see The Diamond King."

"Now that I said be available, whatcha' you goin' to do?"

"Be available when you call baby," she acquiesced. Sounding sexy and cordial. I disconnected the call and headed in the direction of my ex-stepson and his thieving ass basketball-dribbling friend. I still haven't received a call from

Ice which is just weird to me. Before we crossed the line, she would have called me just to talk and make sure I made it home, or to my destination in one piece. I'll give her a call if she doesn't call me, after my affairs for the night have been taken care of.

I went through the back entrance unchecked and posted up in VIP. I ordered a few bottles even though I don't drink. It was the cheese for the mouse trap to cut the head off a rodent. While sitting there texting Church, verifying his whereabouts, the sparkling bottles rolled up as the team of 12 topless ladies came through like disciples carrying the spirits of the night. Just like clockwork, the mice and rats came for the cheese in the trap. They drank and partied while I ate a few hot wings, well done, all flats as energy before starting my hunt.

"Help yawl selves; it's a celebration," I said with my arms spread wide like the pope on the balcony.

"We got Mr. Seldom Seen, but still owns the team in the VIP tearing it down early. Save some bottles for me!" the D.J. shouted. I nodded nonchalantly at the recognition.

"Also," he continued, "The Diamond King will be in the building tonight, ladies and gentlemen.

We about to turn all the way the fuck up. Smoke your smoke, sip your sip, and pop pills, not pistols. It's a real nigga celebration or should I say coronation tonight." The DJ hyped the majority female crowd who got in free before the cover charge began. Pace was going to be loud and flashy with his newfound wealth. I know his type. His mother probably warned him, but I'm sure that tough shit in him allowed him to listen. Looked at my watch, it's 11:45 p.m., way earlier than I usually show up to any event. Notifications on my phone informed me that everything was on the way to being back in order. I checked the entrance for a king and a thief. He probably will be backstage flossing. I waived over a curvy yellow bottle girl and whispered what I wanted to know while sliding her a few blue faces and proceeded to locate the thief with this shiny gold bottle in my hand. Around the corner, I located his Crown Crew relaxing, drinking, dropping tobacco on the floor as they rolled up some bullshit smelling like they needed a new weed man.

"Looks like it's perfect timing," I said to myself.

The first guy's back was turned as he stood posted on the wall. "Thump!" I swung hard like trying to kill a fly in midair, right in the back of the head where his fitted cap used to be. In shock, his body seized before collapsing in front of me, crashing to the ground. The goofy to my left wearing the wife beater with the fading tattoos, stood 6'5 and wasn't about that life at all. His eyes twinkled as he tried to posture and deter me with a look that was laughable. Overly anxious, I swung too wild and missed as he weaved to his left. More patient this time, I doubled back and hit him flush on the jaw catching his unguarded chin with the follow up.

"What you hit me for? I didn't do nothing!" he said. His innocence fell on deaf ears. Like my parents back in the day, I continued to strike.

"You ain't gonna do nothing else," I chastised.

With all the commotion, most of his entourage vacated like roaches with the lights on. Leaving nothing but one guy and two groupies, he told them that they didn't have to leave. His remaining protection lifted his shirt to show his gun. It was too shiny, so I knew it hadn't seen any wartime. A hard left hook to his eye with my chin tucked and on my toes; I circled to the right. Following up with a hard-right hook to the mouth, he grimaced. Two hard, body blows and a strong uppercut to the chin, and it was lights out. He managed to hit me under the eye, but that wasn't shit for this light work.

The basketball dribbler set there in aww with his weak mid-range shot and shitty handles having ass. The undersized point guard had no chance to make it to the league even though I always told him to never give up and keep practicing.

"Nigga, you know why I am here," I said before I slapped fire out of his ass. "I know you a bitch. You didn't come looking for me after what I did to your thieving ass momma." I slapped him again, as all of the pretend man came draining out of him.

"Ooh!" The cheerleaders said in unison.

"My sister set everything up. She said you would be an easy lick," Pace whimpered.

"You ain't got no sister. Nigga, I know you."

"She's my half-sister. We got different daddies," he muttered, reminding me that I didn't know him that much at all.

"Who the fuck is yo' sister? What's her name?.....What's her name?" I demanded with his designer shirt tearing under my clinched fists. He gave it up without hesitation; a captain who refused to go down with his ship.

"Sh..Sh...Shona," he whimpered with a studder. She knew you from some pa….pa..parties," he continued.

"Damn!" The room started to spin a little bit. The Club queen out charmed me, I thought to myself. Gritting my teeth in disbelief, all I saw was darkness. I pounded him with my bare hands crashing down on his face. Repeatedly, like I did the monster in the woods, the skin on my knuckles ripped as I tore through his flesh. Pace laid there unconscious. I grabbed the top of the broken bottle, jammed and twisted it in his shooting hand destroying the ligaments with every twist.

I confiscated the two cheerleader's cellphones and exited out of the back door. The Diamond King was next, but he ain't arrived yet for his fair share. My shirt slightly wrinkled with blood blended in the fabric, I felt different as if the part of me was buried somewhere suppressing my rage. For the times I smiled when I didn't want to, and I just maintained my composure. When I decided to be diplomatic, although the times clearly called for war. Shona Evans pussy was good, but it damn sure ain't worth millions.

I hurried back to the truck. Police cars and ambulances sped in the opposite direction towards the location where I took my reparations. While I thought about Shona, a Chrysler 300 with big rims and tinted windows crept towards me. The passenger side windows were down and them young niggas had those tools out. If it wasn't for them shouting instead of shooting me, I would have been dead for sure. Military guns with the 100 round drums hanging out, I ran. Ducking and keeping my head low and my eyes up as they started letting off rounds rapidly. I didn't even have time to bust back, too busy trying to maneuver. I dropped the stolen cell phones and crushed them with my hurried steps inadvertently. The assassins were sweeping their arms side to side hitting everything in sight. Car alarms went off, windows busting, tires flattening, and people screaming.

"Thunder raining from the sky as the bullets fly!" The music turned up but I stayed low to the ground as they drove by. The unmistakable sound echoed as the chopper bullets roared through the air cutting down anything in its path. Spent shell casings poured onto the concrete, bouncing and rolling before coming to a final rest.

"The Diamond King, muthafucka," said one of the amateur hitters. The studio gangsters had been watching too many movies. As soon as they stopped to reload, I crotched down behind a blue

Benz riddled with bullets. My faithful 9mm with hollow points would do the trick since I had aim. Every shot straight through the open windows on the passenger side ripped the souls out of my enemies. Unable to return fire, they drove away crashing into three cars in the process.

I expected no greater outcome, but to survive and defeat my enemies. I headed back to my truck parked one street over unscathed with my black gun in hand. This time, I was aware of my environment.

Chapter 2

Notifications went off on my phone from Instagram and TikTok, because someone liked a pic and there was a message in my DM's. The Diamond King liked a pic of me and Stormy chilling on vacation in Turks and Caicos. She was looking good in that two piece. I ain't mad at the taunting boy king, because I knew his time would be up very soon. The DM was this clown too, "Right Back Ain't Cheatin', he wrote." I didn't reply. He got the wrong one, thinking this is a game.

Helicopters and police were all around the club, making it impossible to stay and wait for the self-proclaimed Diamond King. I headed towards my westside spot to change clothes and wait on Church to eliminate Tags. The Bishop will be used to eliminate the Club Queen. Sounds like church service is in order this Sunday. Plus, I need to make sure that greedy bastard does exactly what I told him to do.

Finally, back at my building, I immediately noticed that Ice's pink truck ain't there and my Buick tires were flat. "Who the fuck been over here fucking with my shit! If it ain't one thing it's another," I said to whoever might be listening.

Upstairs on the top floor, my door was slightly cracked. I slowly wiggled my way through the partially opened door with my pistol cocked and ready. I'm shooting anything that moves, whether it's a curtain or anything else. Stormy's large suitcase with a note attached sat in the hallway between the living room and the front door. "Stormy are you in here? Who the fuck in here!" I yelled, impatiently.

I rummaged around the entire place with my pistol in the ready position. No one answered. I methodically began searching for the two remaining lofts. Knocked on Ice's door, but there wasn't any answer. Headed to the bottom floor, and everything was how it was supposed to be. I returned upstairs and checked the luggage for what I assumed to be my cash, not even thinking about if it was rigged to explode. I opened it and the cash was neatly packed in bundles. The note was typical Stormy, wanting me to forgive her for her bullshit, her constant mistakes and blah… blah… blah. I tossed it to the side like an empty birthday card. I sat on the couch exhausted momentarily dozing off.

Awakened by my phone vibrating from notifications and text messages, "R.I.P. The Diamond King."

"What the fuck!" I am shocked, but not saddened as the information and posts go up and down my news feed on Facebook, Instagram and TikTok. There was a candlelight vigil at the club where I was just blazing under pressure. Fans cried and were comforted by other fans. Teddy bears and empty bottles of liquor helped celebrate the memorial along with framed pictures. A partial video of the shootout was being broadcast all over the internet, but no suspects were identified.

No witnesses were willing to speak with police. A suspect matching my description was broadcast, but the information was so vague that it could fit almost anyone. I wondered if he was in the car during the drive-by. I don't remember seeing him, but hell, I don't even know what any of the other guys looked like. I just remember the barrel of the gun pointed toward me, the flash, the bullets whizzing by, glass crashing at my feet and people running for cover in panic. My hands and clothes still smelled of gun powder. Gotta get the details regarding this situation, because I don't know if his body is on my gun or not. The crashed Chrysler was still where I last seen it, but the boy king is covered up with a sheet and taped off in a different location.

Before allowing myself to believe the rumors that often circulate faster and further than the truth, I knew I must reach out to someone, but who? Angie!...... Ignoring her text, I just simply Facetimed her. She is a fan, and well, she does always know the 411 about something. She should be a gossip columnist or spy in the time of war.

"Hey, Angie. what's up baby?"

"What's up. Ain't you heard. They killed The Diamond King! This shit fucked up. People saying it was the police or some niggas from Chicago that he had a rap beef with. I'm not sure though."

"What happened? I'm glad you didn't go to that concert and get hurt baby," I said in the most considerate way possible.

"The concert never happened. Some niggas got to fighting inside the venue and then it spilled over outside the club. It was a big shoot out, and people were saying that they had K's and shit. It was like a war zone!" Angie spoke as if she was reporting live from the scene.

"Damn, for real? That's wild! That's why I try to stay in my own lane. Liquor and niggas don't mix," was all I could muster up.

"His boys in the 3 hunnid' got shot up trying to shoot at somebody. Supposedly, some guys that they were beefing with inside the club. Two of them died and the driver is in critical condition."

"Where was the Diamond King?" I asked, thinking of my missed opportunity.

"They said he was on his way there. When he arrived, he was trying to see what happened to his boys, but him and the police got into it. But some people are saying them Chicago niggas caught him lacking and lit him up. My girl Samantha still down there lighting candles and going live. She said it is lit. People are just playing his songs and chillin.' The Making of a Diamond King is that cut."

Angie needs a career change, "Damn, I hate that happened to him. I've known him ever since he was a young boy."

"I know you used to fuck with his momma. You stayed fucking they momma's. You was like a coach having them hoes trade pussy for the promise of starting positions on the team for their sons. HAHA!" She busted out in laughter.

"Girl you crazy. It wasn't nothing like that. If stuff like that happened, it wasn't me."

"What was it like then? Never mind, you just gonna' lie anyway. What time you comin over? You gonna let me taste it? My mouth horny. You make me feel like I'm begging," she quickly went from mourning to complaining.

"If I was making you beg, you would know the difference," I said, breaking up the monotony.

"How so?" Angie asked curiously as usual.

"Because, you would be on your knees begging with a collar on your neck while I pulled on the leash."

"You a freak, but that did make my pussy throb and jump a little bit," she admitted.

"If it only jumped a little that means you need to listen a little harder."

"Naw, it just means that this pussy full grown, and you need to do more than just bark at it to make her really purrrrrr!" she countered.

"Yeah, aight'. We gone see. Have you heard from Tags, with your grown pussy havin' ass?"

"Tags? I don't fuck with him like that. He promised he could get a few of my girls the hook up on some real estate on the low, fix credit scores, and different stuff like that, but he never came through. I damn near had to go to blows with one of my girls because of it. Why you askin' me about Tags lying ass?"

"Just curious. You know your ass be knowing too much about everybody business," I reminded her with sarcasm.

"I can't help it that people feel comfortable sharing their secrets with me. For the most part, their secrets are safe."

"I'm on my way over. I hope you can keep a secret," I joked, knowing she can't.

"What kind of secret do you want me to keep?" she questioned innocently.

"That I'm putting a passion mark on your booty."

"HAHA, your crazy nasty ass. I ain't never had a passion mark on my booty before. Which cheek? The right or the left?" Angie turned to show each.

"Both. What else you ain't never did?" I asked.

"You know I don't do too much. I'm innocent."

"Mmmm, hmmm. You ain't gotta be innocent for me, just willing baby."

"I hear you, now come get this pressure off me. I need some of your stress reliever," said the blunt seductress.

"I'm on my way over. I can't stay too long. I got to go to church in a few hours."

"Church, church or drunk ass Church?" she asked.

"Bishop Blessing's church? Put some respect on my fam name," I reminded her.

"HAHA! Nigga quit lying. You don't go to church. My bad bae, you know I was playing about your friend. That's the church Turtle and 'em go to."

"That's right. They do go there, but I do go to church for funerals and weddings, and tomorrow it's for both" said the voice of vengeance.

"Bae, you crazy. I'm finna' get in the shower. My door will be unlocked."

I wiped my face with ice cold water to wake myself up before heading over Angie's house. I looked in the mirror and plucked a few random gray hairs appearing in my beard. The scratch on the side of my face is one of the many signs of tonight's altercation. The bags are becoming more apparent by the minute and proof that my vacation has been anything but paradise like I thought it would be. My arms were scratched and scarred; my knuckles bruised with a chunk of skin missing. "Looks like you been through hella battles," speaking to the man in the mirror nodding my head in response. This shit ain't nowhere near over until I know the truth." My clothes changed and fresh after the much-needed pep talk, I was ready to see what Angie was working with. All that mouth she got; she better be able to back it up.

Chapter 3

I pulled up to Angie's house about an hour or so later: a big white abode at the end of the cul-de-sac with a newly renovated roof and gutters. The porch light was on, and I couldn't help but notice a moth trying to enter the light and bouncing off the bulb. Not to be denied, it continued to try to do the impossible. "I know the feelin," I said to the moth. I crossed the threshold into the living room with a mounted 85-inch T.V. connected to all the hi-tech amenities. Some of Turtle's work without question. All wireless and top of the line. Large sectional couch with both leather and suede, black and burgundy respectively evenly distributed throughout the length of the sectional. The same color scheme was blended well with the rest of the furnishings. The "Footprints in the Sand" poem placed strategically above the couch in the center of the wall. I placed my shoes with the rest of the shoes neatly by the glass and mahogany cabinet before making my way across her soft plush carpet that she freshly vacuumed. The smell of lightly scented candles permeated the airwaves, vanilla and cinnamon reminded me of dessert.

"I see you made yourself comfortable bae," she said, posing at the entrance from the other side of the room. She was fresh out the shower still with a lil' soap on her right shoulder. A fluffy white bath robe wrapped around her doing little to hide them plump breasts that were waiting for me to massage and suck. Her head neatly crowned in a matching towel.

"I felt comfortable when I wiped my feet on the welcome mat. You smell like you're soft and you taste good," I said while licking my lips. "If you get too comfortable you might not want to leave, and I'm definitely soft and tasty baby," she replied.

"Ain't nothing like dessert first, before the main course," I simply assured my hostess.

"The desserts and the main course will be served in the tent outside. Something light with your favorite fruits. We can feed and taste each other. Some drink for me and some drink for you," Angie said like she was fresh out of my cooking class.

"Let me see that magic tent that you got specially decorated."

She led me to the back window to view the big blue tent that looked like a small mountain standing alone in the backyard in between two large trees. Her cheeks jiggled slightly as she walked looking tantalizing and teasing me with every step. I smacked her soft ass and gave it a firm squeeze like fresh fruit at the market.

"Damn, that's a nice tent, shid that's plenty of room to do whatever." I looked directly into it from the window through the sky roof opening above. My hand was still massaging her soft, thick cheeks as I was anticipating tonight's adventure.

"Whatever is definitely on the menu tonight," she reminded me, smiling and batting her eyes flirtatiously. "I'm going to put on something more comfortable for the occasion. I'll be right back."

I stared out of the window at the magnificent tent under the stars in the backyard. Jolted back into the moment by a knock on the door, I turned my attention from the tent to the other end of the house, preparing myself for some circus shit. "Somebody at the door!" I shouted up the stairs, but she didn't respond quickly enough. With my burner in hand, I stalked the door to investigate. After a night like this, I can't afford to allow my guard to be down. A female with a dark colored dress, and a yellow flower pinned to her left side stood anxiously at the door. She was pacing in place hurriedly. I waited patiently to see if she came alone, or made any sudden moves. Her body would be riddled with bullets without me even opening the door. She knocked again this time with more force.

"Who is it?" I said, demanding the identification of the intruder.

"Who at the door?" The words came from behind me before the mystery lady could reply.

"I ain't hip. Some chick with a flower on her dress," I shouted back over my shoulder.

"It's me, Samantha. Girl, open the door. I gotta use the bathroom," she said in a frenzy.

"Go ahead. That's my girl Sammy. Whatever you do, don't call her Sam. She hates it."

"I hate when people show up unannounced. What is she doing here this late anyway?" I questioned about the potential cockblocker.

"She don't live too far from here. She probably stopped by to tell me about what went down at the concert," Angie explained.

"Hurry up before I pee on myself!" the uninvited guest complained with attitude. I cautiously opened the door with my right hand slowly to reveal the full picture of the woman that stood in front of me. The pistol was tucked behind my back in my left hand. Her face had a unique look for sure, but her body was something she took pride in. Her form laid comfortably under the fabric as she hurried by.

"Hey, how you doing? I'm Sammy. I didn't mean to interrupt. I gotta use it."

"Hey, what's up Sam? My bad, Sammy." She looked at me and smiled.

"Girl, I got company. I didn't know you were coming by. Take them shoes off," my hostess said to her pissy friend.

"I couldn't make it home. That's that liquor comin' out of me, girl," the lightweight admitted. She hurried to the bathroom, but it wasn't too fast to where I couldn't notice her ass, soft and round like a bubble. It aroused me slightly. She was in tuned with her femininity. It exuded sexuality. I knew I wasn't feeling this vibe alone.

"Come on bae. Let's head to the tent," Angie said now wearing a gold sheer negligee with furry slippers. We walked through the patio door and down the steps of the large wooden deck that was added with the rest of the renovations. Dimly lit just enough to see each step-in front of me, the lightning bugs and crickets sang as to announce our arrival. There was a small mixed fruit tray and a black bottle of champagne chilling in an ice chest. The faux mink blanket was neatly placed over the thick air mattress.

"I got you a case of these ginger beers that I saw you drinking before," my bae for the day announced.

"Attention to detail. I like that," I said with pleasure.

"What else you like?"

"Getting what I want without asking, and asking for it and getting it?" I riddled.

"Which do you like the most?"

"You pay attention to details. You tell me?" I said as she blushed.

"You.... too silly. I love a man with a sense of humor." She placed a chilled grape in my mouth that I crushed under my teeth; then the sweetest pineapple chunk I ever tasted.

"Your turn," I whispered. I grabbed a cherry, touched her nose with it. Tapped it on her tongue, teasing her lips rubbing them with the ripe red fruit. Directed her with my hand to look up and open wide. Dangled the cherry above her before placing it slowly in her mouth. She tied the stem of the cherry with her tongue, putting her mouth skills on display.

"Damn, I see what that mouf do!"

"I'm gonna show you better than I can tell you."

I massaged her nipple with watermelon not even waiting for her to undress. Her nipple played peek-a-boo as she became more aroused.

"Look what you did," she said.

I switched to the other nipple, so it wouldn't get jealous. The sweet ripe watermelon wedge fit well into her mouth. Angie sucked on my finger and tickled the tip with her tongue.

"Lay on your stomach," I whispered as she assumed the position. I picked up a cube of ice from the champagne bucket. Secretly enjoying the coolness on my scarred hand, the ice cascaded down her spine. It slowly melted as it met her skin adding more shine to her tattoos.

"Ooh, it's cold...... but it feels so good," she whispered in a pleasurable moan. I slapped her ass firmly forcing echoes to ring throughout the tent. I heightened the experience blowing cool breath onto her wet skin. The cold water dripped between her cheeks as I massaged her pussy with my middle finger. Soft bites increased the sensation. My finger turned in her, going deeper, and summoning her to come closer. Her back arched. Her walls, wet and warm, contracting as I slowly pulled my finger halfway out continuously. I teased her soul to the brink of climaxing.

"Turn over," I ordered, deepening my voice. I licked and pinched her left nipple, and her legs formed a figure four while her body tightened.

"Ooh, yes baby!" she moaned louder as my finger massage worked wonders on the narrow pathway to her G-spot.

Above my head, I felt somebody watching me. I turned around slowly not making any sudden moves. Through the opening above I could see her friend looking down at us, pleasuring herself. Once eye contact was made, she started to enjoy herself more. Now, I began watching the girl with the bumblebee booty dance and please herself with one leg on the ledge of the bay window and the other foot planted firmly on the floor of the dining room. I planted soft kisses on Angie's lower back, slowly kissed on her neck, and nibbled on her ear. She squirmed helplessly on the ground ready for me to place myself inside of her womb, teasing her to the point where nothing else would do.

"Put that hard dick in me, bae. I gotta feel you! Right now."

With pleasure, I bent her over, no longer paying any attention to the friend above, and no longer mesmerized by the dancing night bee. Entering her fully erected as the veins on my dick came in full contact with her wet walls, I fit her like this is where it belonged. The missing piece of the puzzle. My hands, strongly, on her shoulders, I dug deep inside of her body. Gentle is really what gets her off. Slow is really what makes her wet. Firm is what makes her submit, obeying to my commands without saying a single word. I mounted her from the side with bites and soft kisses on her lips. I pulled her closer to me while getting deeper inside of her wetness. Her fruit pie spilling onto my thighs like a cup overflowing. Warm and sweet, I can taste it in the air. The head of my dick swelling up inside of her. Deep long strokes stretched her walls making the fit snugger.

"Don't come yet," she said softly as she looked back at me. Slowing down my pumps, pulling my hard-swollen dick from the inside of her, I laid on my back looking through the roof for her peeping friend that was no longer in the window. Angie slowly sucked on me while positioned on her elbows with her ass in the air looking at me shyly, but confidently. Her tongue danced on my tip teasing me. My body jerked resisting the strong urge to release it in her mouth.

"I want to taste some," the peeping friend said from the entrance of the tent exposing her tongue ring for the first time. Standing in the nude, the small chested woman with the strong sex vibe made her way inside. No one stopped her. She crawled behind Angie gulping her smacking her lips. Angie moaned on my dick every time she took me into her mouth. No longer on her elbows, her hands were fixed into the fabric of the planetary blanket as she began to grind on her friend's face.

"Girl, come taste this hard ass dick with me," Angie suggested.

"Say no more. I can't wait to work my black girl magic on it," her naughty friend said.

"Naw, don't use no hands. All mouth…we grown. Spit on this dick and lick it off," I ordered. They obeyed taking turns spitting on it and sucking it off. "There yawl go, just like that," I said. They exchanged kisses amongst each other as if they did this before. Bonded by soul ties. Each with a side, planting kisses. Then sucking on my bell head, sending chills up my body, gritting my teeth, and gripping the blanket. It's taking everything in me not to shout to the heavens. The double team was working, but I be damned if I tap out. I changed positions so I can have the upper hand, heart racing and feeling good to be alive. I mounted the voyeur friend grabbing her waist like a silver back gorilla.

"Beat this naughty, good pussy up. Gimme that wrecking ball!" she said, taunting me with her tongue ring. Angie underneath her with her mouth open ready to catch the fresh squeezed juice. Stuffing myself inside of the petite woman hammering her soul, sent shock waves through her body.

"More!" she screamed. "More!" she demanded. Her narrow walls began to open as her juices poured. Angie licked my balls while Samantha licked on Angie. I just continued to pound away, giving everything I had. She was taking it and demanding more of it. I removed my hands from her waist as she winded her hips and crashed down on my hard erection. The force caused ripples in her ass cheeks. Burying her face inside of Angie, as she took over the show, her small frame fit so nicely between us. We adapted to her rhythm as her pussy was trying to pull the soul out of me. Samantha clinched and gyrated. Some of the best pussy I have ever encountered. Regaining composure like a fighter dazed on the ropes, I grabbed her waist thrusting with everything I had in me. She looked back at me in ecstasy, with her palms gripping Angie's thighs.

"This pussy loves that dick. Yes, here comes another one," said the voyeur. I slapped her ass, and she came again, instantly arousing me to another level. I grabbed her shoulders, dug all the way to the bottom of that deep wet pussy. I felt her pussy lips swelling as I continued to give her what she craved.

I pulled out just in time. They both came and drank from my fountain together without a drop being wasted. My arms rested on my side while Samantha churned my dick like a pepper grinder sucking on the head further weakening me. Her eyes focused staring through me getting every drop.

"Can you go again, or do you need to rest first?" Bumble bee booty wasn't ready to quit, and I was on my knees looking for the soul that she sucked out of me.

I laid down planning to recuperate, but they swarmed me. Angie sat on my face looking in the direction of the soul stealer as she straddled me rocking forward and backwards doing a ritual to resurrect my erection.

Chapter 4

Pouring rain awakened me as it tumbled down on the roof of the tent. The breeze was gentle and calming but enough to get me to my feet. I tapped Angie on the head to get her up.

"What's wrong?" she said in a groggy voice.

"Time to get up sleepy head," I replied in a voice just as groggy.

I scanned around for the voyeur, and she wasn't nowhere to be found. We walked slowly up the steps. My legs cramping, I was half-dressed walking into the dining area where I could smell coffee brewing and breakfast cooking.

"Morning yawl, I had a blast last night. Thanks for allowing me to be a part of the festivities," the tongue tangler said.

I looked at that happy broad. I was tired than a muthafucka that I didn't even respond. As I made my way to the bathroom so I could take a piss, I looked in her medicine cabinet to make sure she ain't got no crazy pills, disease pills or no pregnancy pills. Nothing in there but the regular stuff. It was 8:30 a.m. and I felt like I hadn't slept in days. I wiped the toilet seat of any miss aimed drip and headed to the kitchen.

"Girl, Mario was blowing me up last night. He be calling me too much. He needs to get him some friends that he can do stuff with cause' I can never have no fun. Look at all these missed calls," said the voyeur. She turned her phone with a crack on the screen towards us to show proof.

"Hey, Angie. You need to get dressed. You riding over to the church with me," I reminded her interrupting the show and tell.

"Church? You was serious about goin'. After last night, I will be nervous thinking that bishop is talking 'bout me."

"Girl, cut it out. I'mma head to my house. I will be back at about 10:00 a.m. to getchu," I told her.

"You don't want breakfast before you leave?" said the super freak and subpar cook with the lumpy grits.

"Naw, Sammy. I don't eat it if Gold Label ain't on the table." I headed out the door walking slowly with my shoes in my hand. "Hey somebody pulling up. It looked like the dude on your phone, Sam. Looks like he got a few questions to ask." I slammed the door of the house and headed to my truck. I saw them looking out of the living room window from my rearview mirror for the make-believe stalker that wasn't there. I'm sure Angie called to say I played too much, but I didn't answer. I just continued with my mission. Finally, I got a text from Church saying that he made his move, meaning that Tags had been taken care of, but he will have to have his head for proof.

The traffic was thick for a Sunday morning, and of course, people can't seem to drive in the rain. Accidents everywhere, so I played my mirrors whipping in and out of lanes. I pulled into my west side spot. Still no sign of Ice and no text either. I knocked on the door. Still no response. "Damn, where the fuck she at?" I said to the door. I called her phone heading up to my place, but it went straight to voicemail. "What she on? I know she ain't feeling guilty about yesterday."

I shitted and showered and went right back out. All black and casual. I pulled back up to Angie's house at 10:30 a.m. and she still wasn't ready.

"Girl, come on! We running late."

"I'm coming," she said, finally.

"You probably been coming ever since I left, cause' you should have been ready. I know you ain't been eating them lumpy ass grits."

"HAHA, Nigga them grits still was good" said the chef in training.

I offended her, but she still looked like she wanted to fuck right there in the kitchen. "I will have to invite you over for cooking class, so I can get you together. We can make shrimp and grits."

"No, the fuck yawl ain't! Craft, you better quit playing with me. Come on let's go!" Angie sounded a lil' jealous.

"Oh, now you ready to get up out of here to getchu' some word in your life. Well, yes lawd," I said, mimicking the Bishop. We turned to leave, but not before making eye contact with the third wheel. I knew she would be in touch. By the way she ate her food and licked the spoon.

Once in the truck, I set the mood. Slow music bumped through my surround sound. Time to get some things off my chest. "Take them panties off," I said calmly with the confidence of Teddy P. Angie looked hesitantly questioning me with her eyes. Then eagerly relented tossing her panties in the third row. I rubbed her pretty pussy to the rhythm of the music while the windshield wipers made the tinted view clear. She spread her legs wider, allowing me to touch her properly. The storm brewed from my fingertips. Splashing while rotating my wrist, I turned corners at the same time.

"You make this pussy so wet! I think she really like you, bae," Angie petitioned with her eyes closed. Firm, slow caressing touches stimulated her clit as it slowly began to swell. Once her body started clinching, I stopped and changed the rhythm up allowing the pressure in her orgasm to build. Her swelling clit sensitive to my touch. Her soft nipples hardened poking through the lace bra and blouse. "Why you doing me like this? You teasing me. You ain't right for that," she said, but I continued anyway.

"Shut that ass up and open wider." I patted and rubbed that pussy at the red light while she fingered herself vigorously. Her feet were firmly on the dash, damn near kicking the steering wheel as she rocked back and forth.

"OH, OH SHiiiiiiiiTTT! Damn your fingers are like magic, baby. That's a hell of a way to start the morning."

"You got my fingertips all wrinkly from that water flow." I licked my fingers enjoying the taste.

"My pussy is sweet I can't lie."

"Grab me a wipe out of the glove compartment lil' nasty."

"Hold up, boy. Shit! That hit the spot early," Angie said like she needed a cigarette.

"I know it was better than breakfast." LMAO!

"Shut your hating ass up, Craft," she demanded.

Chapter 5

We arrived at The Lord's Cathedral. You could hear the music rocking from the inside. We trickled in with the rest of the late folk dressed to impress.

"Girl, Sister Lewis told me that they ain't collecting tithes or offerings this morning cause God told Bishop not to. Plus, I heard he gave his Rolls Royce away," the lady with the bad weave said.

"Whaaaaaat! Are you serious? He probably lost it gambling. Thank the Lord, cause' I can use this money to get caught up on some bills," cheered the slightly older lady.

"I'm going to the hairdresser, so I can get me some new hair. I done had this in for two months. I was going to wait until next check, but I done called Theresa down at the shop and made my appointment for first thing Tuesday morning."

"Don't you have to work?" the older lady reminded her.

"Girl, they won't be seeing me. The Lord told me to take off and enjoy myself. HAHA." Her laughter was fit only for the outdoors.

"Ooh chile', I know that's right!" Their two hands collided in agreement.

We were finally instructed to a seat by the short round semi-curvy lady with the thin mustache. She barked orders with a handful of pamphlets. Her all-white uniform was freshly pressed with a smudge of brown makeup on her collar. Two rows ahead of us to my left, I noticed Martha and Turtle standing enjoying the choir, singing along. As soon as Martha turned her head in our direction, I placed my hand on Angie's thigh nearly up her skirt. Martha tried to hide the fact that she was probably turned on nudging Turtle in disgust, so he could look over our way. I gave him a head nod and a smirk while Angie and I waived. This is going to be a wonderful service. I can see the flames coming out of his eyes. I laughed at his big lame ass.

"Good morning, saints" said the Bishop dawning a white robe trimmed boldly in purple and gold. He sweated profusely, wiping his head with a bright white hand towel that laid conveniently on the elaborate crystal podium with the flat screen in the front projecting a live video feed of the service. There were so many monitors throughout the massive cathedral that it almost gave the appearance of a sports arena.

"Good morning, Bishop," was the response from everybody, but me. Even Angie chimed in on queue.

"Today, I will be delivering a word that has to do with faith. For faith without works is dead.

"Amen. Amen, Bishop!" his flock responded.

"I know summa ya', is tired this morning. It's written all over ya' faces. Strip clubs and lemon pepper wings. Casinos and house joints. Orgies and carrying on. You're in the right place for deliverance! I used to be out in the world before this word got into me. I feel like having some church this morning. Amen?

"Amen, Bishop!"

"Amen!" but this word. I'z says this word, will wake up the soul. This word will wake up the dead like it did for Lazarus."

"Yes, bishop. Say that. Say that," said a woman with a tight red dress.

"Praise God for the Bishop. Amen. He so anointed," an elderly woman reminded us.

"See faith is like walking down the steps in the dark. Sometimes you get nervous. Sometimes you get frightened. But my God, can I get a witness? My God didn't give us the spirit of fear. He gave us the spirit of resolve. The spirit to fight. The spirit to walk down those steps with no lights. Just faith the size of a mustard seed. That's what the words says. You are a child of the only living God and He and only He will guide you to where you need to be. You feel uncomfortable even though you know the stairs are there, but sometimes it's just by faith you must courageously step down those stairs even if you can't see them."

"Amen, Bishop!" the crowd shouted in unison.

"Now, I know it's summa dem college educated folk, or over thinkers in here and they wondering why I ain't talking about walking up them steps. I know peanut head, Tyrone, is one of them. He is a smart ass; I mean aleck just like his daddy was at his age. Sorry saints, that slipped out just like some of yawl didn't make it home cause yawl slipped in...... Amen."

"Amen, Bishop" the crowd echoed in the midst of laughter.

The reason I ain't talking about walking up the steps is because the fear of falling up the stairs in the dark isn't as bad as falling down the stairs in the dark. Sister Williams stumbled down the steps last week breaking her hip, so I know what I'm saying is real. There are examples in the word and in the world. Amen? The Lord is them steps. If we lose sight, we are subject to fall."

"Amen, Bishop."

"Since we ain't collecting any tithes today, the Lord put it on my heart to give up some free game. Free game Sunday. Oh, the football team might not win on Sunday, amen?"

"Amen, Bishop. I know that's right!" the sharp dressed Deacon pronounced with a foot stump.

"You spent your last on that same number for years and you still ain't hit it yet. Can I get a witness? Oh, yawl quiet when it comes to them numbers. Pick 3, Pick 4, Pick 5, Midday, Evening, 50 cent straight, and $1 Box. Hallelujah! You gotta play the organ on that, Roscoe! But this game right here you can't do nothing but hit with it. You can't do nothing but win with it. My God is bigger than any Powerball or Mega millions. Bet it all on him, and watch your life turn around. Before I get out of here, I want to remind yawl that Big Barbs got that fish special going and they use fresh grease down there you no summa deez folk use that bad grease that give you the bubble guts."

The congregation laughed with some shouting out the names of the guilty parties.

"There yawl go being messy, Bishop winked. I ain't saying no names."

"You know we got to go to Big Barbs to grab a plate. They got them butterflied jumbo shrimp that be straight fire," Angie said.

"I knew you was gonna want some. That's all you eat, that and dick. LMAO!" I said.

"Boy, I'm ready to run it back. You ain't scaring nobody. You think you a pussy bully, but I'm good and ready lil daddy."

"You ready with help. HAHA! Yeah, don't get to perpin' now," I told her, nodding and smiling.

Turtle saw me near the water cooler while he was holding his wife's hand. He was dressed in a new pale gray suit with a red bowtie like something a teacher would wear. His shoes: brown and shaped like 2 big wooden boxes, which I noticed more as he clunked towards me.

"Hey man. That's foul you been dealing with my sister. We were like brothers," Turtle whined.

"Worry about who your wife is fucking. My business don't concern you," I said. "What does concern me is those contracts to remodel multiple commercial properties."

"Yeah, what about them?" he questioned nonchalantly with his chest in the air.

"What about them? I'm taking them and if you have a problem with it, yawl can have yawl funeral in this same church that they married yawl in. Have that paperwork for me first thing in the morning. If I have to come looking for you, you better not let me find you."

Stunned, he stood there speechless, almost as if I smacked him in front of his woman. "You gonna let him talk to you like that?" said his wayward wife with the shiny blue dress that was a few sizes too small.

That business handled, I headed to chat it up with Bishop. I guess Angie was still mingling. If she ain't where I can find her, she gonna be needing a ride. After all of the hand shaking and church hugs, I met the Bishop in his office.

"Hey Bishop. Thanks for the free game," my delayed rebuttal laced with sarcasm. "I need to know where Shona's been hiding. She hasn't been home in days. Have you seen or heard from her?"

"No brother, I have not. Again, I apologize for the issues with the trust accounts. I will take over the responsibility from now on."

"This is bigger than those accounts. This is about principle. She should not have been able to infiltrate so many levels of security so easily. How in the fuck did you allow her to get access?"

"She got access from you, at least that's what her momma said. Someone she knows gave her some information regarding your finances and passcodes. It might have been that lawyer. You know yawl niggas love trusting white folk with yawl money. It's like pulling teeth trying to get the

Lord's 10 percent out of ya's," Bishop complained, sucking his teeth with his feet on his desk.

"Are you saying Dick did it, or are you speculating?" I pried.

"I'm saying sister Shona is a fine young woman and she knows how to use her charm to get what she wants. She's a gift and a curse, that's what I know."

I left the bishop's office feeling like I knew a little bit more and a little bit less than I did when I first went into the hallow walls of his office. Dick would know the passcodes and have access to valuable information. Shona could have charmed Dick into something without promising him anything. I guess familiarity does breed contempt, as they say. It's time to make a contempt muthafucka real familiar with this side of me. I called up Dick while looking for Angie.

I texted him, "This nigga doesn't answer his phone!" Angie ain't answering her phone. I guess she might have gotten a ride from Turtle. I headed to my truck, and I noticed the different hues of women nicely dressed with their hats on. Reminded me of the times when Big Momma would make us go to church. She would always tap us hard with the funeral fans anytime we misbehaved or fell asleep.

"There she is," I said, eyeing my protégé.

She stood patiently waiting for me, with no attitude she must want something. "I thought you went with Turtle?"

"You ain't getting rid of me that easy, but I'm hungry bae," she said.

"Yeah, I can go for something quick to eat. We gotta get it to go so call it in real quick Angie."

"My phone is dead. I didn't charge it last night. You had me so busy," she admitted with hesitation.

"That was yawl trying to double team me. That was light work for the champ," I boasted. flexing my muscles.

"HAHA, boy you couldn't hang with us. We almost retired you last night," Angie mouthed jokingly.

"Shid, yawl just want a rematch? I already know I puts it down. Yawl had that planned anyway cause you couldn't handle me by yourself."

"Naw not for real, I didn't know she was going to jump in. I came plenty of times thanks to yawl like I was the birthday girl," Angie admitted still exhausted.

Chapter 6

I dropped Angie off and refused her invitation
to run it back this time, because I had too many
things to do today. The roses still yet to bloom
from the bushes in front of my building. A silk
scarf like the one Stormy had that day was stuck
on a bulging branch. You can still smell the scent
of her perfume as the scarf danced in the wind. I
didn't even bother to grab it. I refused to
remember any more of our times together. Hoping
it would just fly away like a balloon at a funeral.
No sign of Ice's truck, but her windows were
closed, and she always left them open on breezy
days like this. Church won't be here for another
hour, if he ain't running behind. Lemme go check
on my baby. This ain't like her to be out of contact
with me for this long, no matter what.

BAM, BAM, BAM! I hammered on the door
with my fist, ignoring the pain. Still no answer. I
turned the key into a whiff of spoilage and rotted
food, furniture ripped up, and broken glass
sprawled throughout the house. "Shit!" My feet
slushed through the pools of water that had nearly
flooded the apartment. "Ice baby, where you at?
Are you ok?" My gun was ready. I passed by the
same unwashed dishes from our breakfast the

other day. Her wilted body lay in the bathtub: cool to the touch, with a light pulse. "Shit! This can't be." I dropped the gun in murky water as I grabbed Ice. She was nude and flimsy. Her lifeless arms dangled in the air. I snatched the shower curtain down to keep her body warm and covered. I began to push death out of her and blow life into her.

"Come on Shanice, breathe for me, baby! You can do it. It ain't your time. Breathe baby…wake up… Shanice, wake up!" I repeated the process of my hands compressing her chest while blowing life into her body 1,2,3,1,2,3…
Her eyes remained stuck in the back of her head while mucus and foam spewed from her mouth. Her body jerked. She coughed and gasped for air. "There go my baby. Get that shit out of you! Come on baby, that's it."

"911, what's your emergency!" I was confused and barely able to speak.
"Help us, PLEASE!" was all I remembered. I don't remember giving the address or anything. I rubbed her head watching her intensely. I held her listening to her faint heartbeat and short breaths.

The sirens echoed in the background like music to my ears. Long kisses on her forehead. I rocked her in my arms, back and forth. "Hold on, Shanice please! Baby, hold on. Who did this to you?" I said, over and over. "Sit right here baby. I'm not going to leave you." I positioned her securely against the tub to retrieve my pistol from the still waters. The murky watery grave was up past my elbow. It was thick with the stench of feces burning my nose. I paddled my arm side to side. "What the fuck is this?" an Ankh that belonged to Ira was recovered with my pistol. I placed the wet costume jewelry in my front pants pocket and my pistol in my inside jacket pocket. The paramedics approached the open door of the apartment hurriedly.

"She's my fiancée. Help her," I said, hoping that would make a difference.

"Sir, we need you to back up. This woman is in bad shape. It is a must that we stabilize her." They continued to work on Ice while the room went black, and the sound was absent. I pounded my fist on the wall in a haze of confusion.

"Why would Ira do this to Ice and where the fuck can I find this giant nigga was my only thoughts."

"She has a pulse," the medic yelled coordinating with his team. They covered her nose and mouth with a mask to supply oxygen. She was barely clinging to life and unaware of her surroundings. I immediately texted Church instructing him to meet me at the hospital ASAP. I rode in the back of the ambulance with Ice, covering her bruised hands with mines. She had purple and blue marks throughout her body, busted lips, and her left eye almost completely shut. Her neck was secured in a brace and her forehead was bandaged in blood-stained gauze covering the gashes. The medic worked frantically while I kept a watch on her vitals. "Sir, everything will be fine. Do you know what happened to her? Sir, can you hear me?" Every bump in the road and beep from the machine brought me deeper into the darkest parts of my mind. I invited hell in, and I intended on giving hell out.

Ira was the second half of the duo. He never came across as a guy who would do something like this. He always praised women with the terms queen and sister, beautiful and everything positive. Being orphaned as an infant by his underaged mother never seemed to change his view on women and their importance in the universe.

"God is probably a woman (he would say a black woman), she is the creator of all we see." He would even have me cleaning up my talk about the bitches and hoes. He basically suggested I focus on the ones that don't exhibit the behavior that I complained about. His advice would stick momentarily, but he never judged my slow progress. He appeared to be a force to be reckoned with on the outside. The ones that knew him or in this case thought we knew him saw he was a gentle giant who literally gave the shirt off his back to a person in need. What would make him turn on her like that, destroying her face, and breaking up her body. Ice has a strong spirit. I know if anyone can pull through it is the wind whisperer. I paced back and forth in the waiting room damn near walking holes through the floor.

"Sorry sir, the baby didn't make it. We tried everything, but the baby died so the mother could live." He placed his wooly hand on my shoulder and continued, "Being in the first trimester that is a very delicate time in the child birthing stage."

"Ice was pregnant? I asked with more curiosity than concern.

"Ice?" the bearer of bad news said looking confused.

"Yeah, Shanice Mitchell, ain't that who you're talking about losing their child?"

He looked down on the tablet he was carrying. "I'm sorry sir that's a different patient. I've been up for 37 hours straight. I completely gave you the wrong information."

"Thank God, I said out loud like a defendant in paternity court. I knew for sure that wasn't mines."

"Ok, Ms. Mitchell is still in surgery. Her chances are looking good. We have the best trauma unit in the state working on her."

"What happened to her?" I asked.

"The detectives ordered a rape kit to test for any kind of vaginal bruising or tears. That information is not available yet. But we do know, she suffered significant trauma to the head and stomach area. The defensive wounds on her arms and hands were clear signs that she fought back, and that extra effort quite possibly saved her life."

"What time will she get out of surgery?"

"As long as there are no unforeseen complications, they should have everything corrected in the next few hours."

"Thanks man, I appreciate it," I admitted, extending my scarred hand that he was reluctant to shake.

Chapter 7

Church texted. He was downstairs in the underground parking lot. I headed in his direction noticing a nurse smiling at me trying to give me some play with her eyes. My best friend almost got killed and I wasn't there to protect her was the only thoughts that I entertained. Why didn't I just call instead of waiting for her to get in contact with me. I know she knows I love her; that's the first thing I will tell her when she wakes up. The elevator moved slowly buzzing as it skipped passed every floor. The smell of the hospital lingered with a mix of excessive cigarette smoke. Large yellow letters and numbers were embossed on columns informing me where I was. The residue of dampness left by the rain gave off an eerie vibe. The intuition that my mother always spoke of having as a child kicked in. It was like I was feeling danger. The hair on the back of my neck stood up. I slowed down my walk as I passed column P34 where a rusted, red Durango rested. I took cover. The clacking of dressed shoes echoed from the distance coming in my direction in a cool deliberate pace. The walking shadow was familiar to me. It was none other than Tags wearing the diamond and ruby pinky ring that belonged to

Church. The sparkle was undeniable. The fedora and shades and the profile were the trademark of the man whose head was supposed to be in a box, completing a contract and ending an era.

I stood up fuming, "Where the fuck is Church?"

"Church's head is in this box that was meant for me. You ain't the only clever nigga. I was onto him at the party back at Turtles' house. He slipped up and looked at his phone. Then he looked back up at me right before walking out to talk to you by the pool. I ain't no dumb nigga by any stretch. I had a couple of my peoples' follow him and let me know his whereabouts. He was laid up with hoes getting drunk instead of sobering up for the mission. The people that you have on your side are the reason for your downfall. I shot the shooter. That girlfriend of yours is a lil' feisty, bitch. She didn't want to let me know where you were. These paws tore into her. She cut my face with a broken queen from the chess board. My momma gonna be pissed." He lifted his shades revealing the gash under his eye. "I was waiting by the door hoping you would come on in running around like a chicken with your head cut off while I brutalized your bitch."

"Yo weak ass been really busy I see," I roared barely maintaining my composure.

"A king stays busy. You was getting too comfortable like the top would always be yours, like I should just get comfortable serving you, shining your muthafuckan' shoes nigga," Tags said, revealing his true motive.

"Tags, I'mma kill your weak ass," I promised, motioning for my pistol. He tossed the box in my direction with the decapitated head revealing its cargo. Immediately when it hit the ground, his pistol soon followed. The area was dimly lit, but I can see by the nose and the hairline that it was Church.

The executioner was executed. The bodiless head came to rest in the puddle of water from the drain above. Shots started ringing out. He didn't give a fuck who was around. "BOOM! BOOM! BOOM!" A young white lady with a stroller nearly got killed if she didn't dive for cover. A bullet grazed me slightly in the arm. "BOOM! BOOM!"

"Nigga, I'm the new king maker in this fucking situation. Now it's your turn to bow and beg." The thirty round clip seemed like he had bullets forever. "BOOM! BOOM!" The shots continued and my ears rung as the shots echoed through the garage. "BOOM! BOOM! BOOM!"

"Freeze! Freeze! Don't you dare move!" commanded the rent a cop with a pistol and a flashlight. He kept shooting. "BOOM! BOOM!" He jumped into a truck and sped out of the parking lot without a single shot being fired back at him.

"Damn, yawl let that muthafucka get away!" Disgusted that he dominated the situation, I wiped my gun down during the commotion and slid it under a car that was gold or tan. The description didn't matter. They can assume that it is his. I didn't fire not one shot.

"Shit!" I thought. Me and Church were supposed to ride back together. I'mma get that muthafucka if it's the last thing that I do. I slipped out of the garage without detection while security checked on the woman and her baby. All these losses I'm dealing with lately have me really thinking about how temporary shit is, people are, and situations.

"Excuse me, sir. We need to talk to you." The words came from a member of the security force as I attempted my smooth get away.

"Damn, I can't even duck rent-a-cops!" I confessed to myself reluctantly. After being questioned for hours and alibied by innocent bystanders, I was finally released. I called an Uber to get back to the penthouse to change my clothes. I will let Unc know the news about Church just in case he doesn't know. The loft is compromised. I'm sure it is still swarming with police and covered in yellow tape. I'm not living there again after what happened to Ice and I'm sure she wouldn't want to move back there either.

Chapter 8

"Traffic is terrible. I wonder what is going on around here?" said Roji the ride share driver trying his best to get five stars. We were a block away from the penthouse when I saw the smoke billowing. The traffic was halted as police began detouring drivers so the fire department and ambulance could easily access the fire.

"Let me out right here!" I said, tipping the driver and hurrying out the car. I ran as fast as I could just to witness my piece of paradise fall from the sky. "GODDAMMIT! This shit is unreal." The windows were busted and shards of charred glass rained down below. The whole top floor engulfed in flames. At this point they were just maintaining the fire to complete rescues. My floor and anything directly beneath will be a total lost. The building appeared to be a fire breathing dragon falling from the heavens as pieces of debris came crashing down onto the pavement. People stood in awe watching my world crumble. Some cheering, and some attentively watching like extras on a movie set. Camera phones replaced traditional panic. The thrill of getting the close up pic or the best video have changed a world full of heroes into a world full of spectators.

"Get back everybody! Get back! This area is dangerous! All of you get back." The orders were repeated by a cop with a bull horn doing his best to control the crowd full of onlookers vying for likes and comments about the fire that they witnessed live and direct on their social media pages. "Yeah, that top floor is a total loss. If there was anyone in there, then they will be looking for remains. There will be no attempt at rescue. The fire was burning too hot and too fast," said the fire chief speaking candidly to a reporter. His face covered in soot and ashes.

A notification came on my phone for a breaking news story with a video of a fire breathing dragon-destroying heaven. The smoke was a thick, grey and black cloud represented everything I was up until today. The heat felt like Armageddon nearly searing my eyeballs while looking up in complete disbelief. My bounce back plan played in my head in slow motion and reverse. If this blow would have come at a time when my money was missing, then I would have been crippled. But I still would have bounced back. I've been broke before, and on the receiving end of a loan before. That shit taught me. The only thing it could instill in a man was to keep his eyes on his empire. To get up no matter what.

Through the crowd, I headed in the direction where I saw the prophet for profit. My life was burning to ashes, and it was broadcasted on the news as the reporter positioned for the best shot. They stood on the borderline of danger, the exact point where falling debris won't kill them, but increase the value of the shot. She stood there looking like a delicate flower with her caramel brown skin and beautiful smile. Much shorter in person, her face was freshly made: a cosmetic mask with beads of sweat on her nose. She was poised trying to hide her insecurities deep down not believing that she was as stunning as she looked.

"Coming to you live from action news, on the scene of this horrific 4 alarm fire. Cut! Let's try it again from over here. I think you can get my angles better."

A black Phantom, like the one I repossessed from the bishop, pulled up beside me. The window came down slowly just like in the movies. It was the boss lady that liked to be dominated. I examined her slender build, bronze skin tanned in the tropics, long black ponytail, and pink and blue frames with rose colored lenses. The stars projected on the interior of her vehicle. "Hey handsome. You're looking like you need a lift."

The white fur shawl rested comfortably over her shoulders. I nodded with my head at my self-proclaimed number 1 fan and patron. The car came to a complete stop. Her driver exited and opened the door for me. Her veneers sparkled as she spoke to me. She extended her arm and placed her hand into my hand. "I'm coming from seeing the play *Hamilton*. It was a phenomenal work! You're looking a little tattered," she noticed as the door sealed us into the futuristic time capsule. "Your hands are cut and bruised," she continued her observation.

"It's been a long day, but I don't have any complaints," I assured her.

"That's a peculiar attitude for someone whose house is bursting in flames. I would be devastated if I lost everything like that."

"Everything isn't lost. I'm rebuilding as we speak."

"You know if you need a place to stay, darling, you can stay at my house near the beach."

"I'm good. I actually need a ride to the hospital to check on my friend."

"No problem. She pushed a button to access the driver attentively awaiting her instructions, "Jesus, drive my dear friend to the hospital."

"Yes ma'me," he replied with a thick foreign accent.

"I hope once everything gets situated, Mr. Craft, that we will be able to see each other again. You are an amazing soul. I enjoy the way you think, the way you know how to tap into me on a spiritual level. I could feel your warmth just by thinking of you. Call me if you need anything. I will be at your service no matter the day or the hour."

Exhausted, I replied, "I definitely will be in touch, beautiful."

"Here is the key to the beach house just in case you change your mind." I reached and she spread her legs revealing that she didn't have on panties. I just leaned my head back to enjoy the ride.

Chapter 9

Back at the hospital, I looked for the room Ice is in. She should be out of surgery by now. The lady at the help desk was nodding off to sleep when I approached her. The heavyset lady had a small bun hairdo, round face, double chin, and her glasses hung halfway off.

"Excuse me. What room is Shanice Mitchell in?" I inquired.

"What was that name again."

"Shanice S-H-A-N-I-C-E Mitchell. Do you need me to spell her last name?"

"No, I have it. She is recovering in ICU, and only family can visit her."

"I'm her husband," I said quickly. I don't know if my left eye jumped, but she didn't believe me.

"MMM… HMMM. Go down the hall, make a left by the cafeteria, and then a right by the next doorway to the elevators on your right. Do you need me to help you find it?"

"No, I got it."

"The room number is 5317."

"Thanks! I'll find it," I said as I hurried away. As I worked my way through the hospital, I couldn't help but notice how cold it was in here. Hospitals smell like there is more death there than life. The hospital was the place big momma came in because of her diabetes and never left. She passed before we could make it to see her for the last time. Thoughts like that didn't belong in my mind right now. Ice was walking out of this place with me as soon as she can. I made a right past the nurses' station following the signs on the wall. Her room was dark. The only light was the machine that pumped fluids in her arm and monitored her vital signs. I pulled up a chair next to her placing her hand into my hand. Her face was swollen and a breathing tube was down her throat. I was speechless. Only thoughts of rage replayed itself over and over. Our revolutionary love hung in the balance, so there was no giving up or giving in. I remember she told me it felt like time stopped when she wasn't around me. Her sentimental instrumentals are what I called those moments when she wanted to be flirty. I wasn't trying to have us feeling no type of way cause we are cool and sometimes I fuck relationships up. Those candid moments between friends loving each other's company, that Love and Basketball type shit in real life.

"You living too fast," she would tell me.

"You'd make a great father. His hair would be curly just like yours."

I wasn't hearing none of that shit, "I can't afford none of those little liabilities right now," I responded.

"They're blessings from God," she would reassure me.

"Yeah, I know. Being a family man might not be my speed. I damn sure don't want to fuck up like my pops. That plays in the back of my head."

"You come off like a perfectionist," Ice said with a look of concern.

"Kids don't ask to be here. I just want to make sure I'm situated. I'm hustling for my legacy."

"That's your same line. Legacy this and legacy that," she argued.

"The minute I'm unable to afford kids then I'm a deadbeat."

"You won't hardly be a deadbeat. You have too much pride to see your child without. Too much integrity to not do your best and provide for your seed. Leave that low hanging fruit alone and you won't be so hesitant."

"Low hanging fruit?" I responded.

"It means..."

"I know what it means. But you're wrong about that. You act like I be just fucking mass hoes or something," I interrupted.

"I never said that, but you do like them ratchets," she blurted out.

"You the ratchetest' chick I know," LOL. She hit me on my chest as I laughed and pulled her closer to me. Those were the times.

My phone rang, "Shit I forgot to turn it off. I walked out of the room to answer the phone. "What up Angie?"

"Hey babe. You ok? Your place is in flames all over the news. What happened?"

"I can't talk right now. I'm at the hospital with Ice."

"Oh ok, I just wanted to let you know that I got a call from Tags which was weird cause you just asked me about him."

"What that nigga say?"

"He was trying to get me to go out for drinks. I told him that I was having company later. Then he started talking about Church being dead. I looked on Facebook and it wasn't coming down my news feed, so I figured he was lie'n as usual."

"Yeah, Church is dead....... my nigga gone."

"Oh, my fucking God! Are you serious!" Angie said between breaths.

"Hell, yeah. He killed my nigga and tried to set me up to kill me in the hospital parking lot," I explained.

"Damn, you done had a few bad days. If you need somebody to talk to, I'm here. You know where to find me."

"I'm more concerned about Ice right now than I am about myself. She ain't have nothing to do with none of this. It's fucked up what happened to Church. That was my brother," I said sadly.

"My condolences, bae. I know you hurtin'. I will leave the porch light on and the back door open."

"I got too much going on right now to be laid up. You just want me to have you coming like hundreds out of that pussy."

"Ooh, you too nasty. Not hundreds coming out my pussy. You'd be big daddy for real."

"You know I'm El Grande Papi," I said with a smile.

"You speaking Spanish now?" Angie asked like she was shocked at my versatility.

"I know a few languages just like you do."

"I don't speak no other language. Are you trying to cap on me nigga."

"That other language you speak is when your eyes talk for your pussy."

"HAHA… boy you crazy."

"Your mouth be drooling with that "I Just Wanna to Suck It" look in your eyes."

"That's how I was looking at you at Turtle's party."

"I know you was. That throat decent though."

"Decent?" Angie replied, thinking that she's Super Head.

"Yeah, you get a D+ for decent."

"My shit way better than decent," Angie said defensively.

"Girl, I'm saying, decent as in good."

"Decent and good ain't the same thing. You just 'a freak nigga."

"HAHA. Girl, you silly as hell. I might let you remind me. Let me get back upstairs. I will hit you up. Thanks for the support and lighthearted conversation, I needed that. Even if it only took things off my mind for a moment."

"You're welcome. I told you, I got you bae."

Chapter 10

I walked a little faster after I heard a mother being consoled after witnessing her child take their last breath. The sound of her voice shrieking crashed down on my eardrums. I ain't finna bury Ice. We will grow old together even if we ain't together. After a few wrong turns, I finally made it back to room 5317. I placed my hand on her shoulder and kissed her on her forehead like I always did. She looked up at me and rubbed her nose on mine. I wasn't trying to do nothing with her for real. She knew almost everything about me. I've revealed things sometimes just to discourage her from feeling me, but it only made her more interested. I haven't felt this guilty in a while. Even with all of the shit that I do, or got going on, guilt was never the response. It was greed.

"My thirst is unquenchable!" I'd always say.

"I can quench your thirst," would be her reply. "Once you stop looking for perfect, you will see your perfect fit."

"I don't believe in the perfect fit. I don't believe in perfect," I corrected.

"Ok, then your best fit," she countered.

"What do you think my best fit is?" I asked.

"A white girl, cause' they will let you do anything you want."

"What? Where you get that from?"

"I'm just saying, a strong woman will give you problems."

"Naw women think being strong is a quality a man looks for first in a woman. I prefer strong femininity not a woman that's a push over like you're trying to say."

"That's how it seems," she griped.

"Maybe you're the one looking at me from a shallow view," I said.

"Maybe everybody ain't perfect like you."

"I just said I didn't believe in perfect," I lectured. Tired of repeating myself.

"You probably don't, but you believe in something close to perfect. You're a narcissist," she continued with her misdiagnosis.

"No, I ain't. I'm that flavor that you crave. What you drool about in your sleep, and the first thing you want to wrap your mouth around when you wake up," I laughed.

"Boy, please! I can't tell that you got it like that in them grey joggers you wearing. That print ain't saying too much," she laughed petting my bulge. "That lilbaby ain't gonna hurt nothing."

The machine beeped continuously as she squeezed my hand tighter as if she didn't want to let go. But deep down, she realized she had to. She began convulsing, eyes began rolling in the back of her head. It sounded like fluids were trying to come up, but the tube prevented them from flowing free. I grabbed the tube thinking it was just in her throat, but it was deep down in her stomach. I banged on the button for the nurse to come in and see what is going on.

"Cold blue! Cold Blue! Sir we are going to need you to wait outside in the hallway," the nurse rushed.

"What's the matter with her?" I stuttered.

"Sir, please. You being here isn't helping at the moment!" she said while ushering me out.

"Ice! Don't leave me! I need you baby," I sobbed.

The tears for Ice and Church finally released. All the buildup poured out at once. I just needed her to be alright and somehow right my wrongs. The only way I knew how was with revenge. Staring at the fire extinguisher in the glass case built inside of the wall instantly reminded me of my penthouse. My clothes were still smoky and torn. My arm was just bruised with a small cut from the stray that Tags shot my way. How did

Church get caught slippin' like that though? I'm not trying to leave before Ice is ok, but I got shit I have to do. The pocket was collapsing. I'm feeling the pressure like a quarterback with the game on the line. I'm not going to leave unless that's the best option for me. I needed to move through this hospital like it was a maze . I finally recognized the nurse with the friendly eyes from the REC. She liked to come in and workout after she worked the late night shift. I spoke with her a couple of times, and we did a few leg days together.

"Hey there stranger. I tried to get your attention earlier, but you looked right through me."

"Yeah, I have a lot going on at the moment. Any word on Shanice Mitchell." I wondered.

"Yeah, she had to be rushed back into surgery. Looks like she has some abdominal hemorrhaging. You definitely don't want fluids to fill up in her lungs."

"Damn, that wasn't what I wanted to hear."

"The good thing is that she is a fighter. Hopefully, she will be fine after this procedure. I am definitely praying for her speedy recovery," she said in a convincing tone.

She grabbed my arm, and I could feel that her concerns were genuine. As much fake shit I've been exposed to, something genuine is definitely what I needed. Our spiritual huddle was interrupted by a charge nurse, a guy well over 6 feet with polished fingernails. "Excuse me," lisped as air passed through his teeth with every word he pushed out.

"Are you Mister Mitchell?" he asked.

"I'm her husband. What's going on with Shanice?"

"The doctor will be over shortly to discuss the situation in full detail."

"Can you at least tell me something," I urged.

"Sir, I can say that she has an infection from a previous medical procedure that somehow opened back up," he said just as loud as he could with his lisp. Smacking his lips with his hands on his hips.

"I appreciate your help," I said reluctantly.

"Anytime," he said as he whisked away.

"Hey, you want to go to the chapel? I can pray with you," said the nurse whose face was familiar, but whose name I couldn't remember.

"Naw, I'm cool. The last time I prayed for someone to live, they died. God already has this figured out either way," I responded. The no-name nurse with good vibes looked at me shocked like she didn't understand the truth in my answer, or like she thought my truth was flawed. Her eyes took a more serious tone like the Jehovah

Witnesses that my daddy used to cuss out for ringing the doorbell too early in the morning.

"I got to get out of here!" I thought out loud while I threw the flimsy cup of hot tea into the wall next to the vending machine of broken promises. My battery was low on my phone. I didn't have a chance to charge it, because my body had been going full speed with little sleep.

"Excuse me sir. Are you Mr. Mitchell?"

"Craft," I corrected. Any word on Shanice?"

"Right now, she is stabilized. She had tearing from scar tissue in her abdominal area. It was from a previous surgery. She must have coughed so hard that it caused tearing."

"So now that it's done, I want to see her. I needed to see her."

"She's not going to be woke anytime soon. If you'd like, you can go home and get some rest and a fresh change of clothes." I caught myself before I said I didn't have a home to go to. I didn't want to complain about losing everything in one night. Before I took the position as a degenerate gambler, I turned and walked away feeling like I could still win it all. This time I'm betting it all on me. Sittin' here ain't helping Ice, I thought. I got to get the revenge that is proper for a King. Anything else would be a letdown.

I'mma get Angie to come swoop me and drive me around for a few, I planned. Her vehicle is more low-key, and I can still play off this burner phone. Ira never showed up and I left him several messages. How is it that I'm here by myself when they are supposedly so close, I wondered. That nigga might not be as innocent as I thought. It's Monday morning, so the shop is closed. He probably will be sleeping in. It was time to give him a wake up! The air outside of the hospital felt good, but the smell was tainted with cigarettes. People in white coats preaching health kill themselves with the same shit they tell us not to do.

Chapter 11

Angie arrived shortly after, looking good. "Morning Angie. You're looking like a Sunday morning breakfast," I said examining her.

"Good morning. I take it you like what you see. I got that bag you wanted me to bring and the gun from under the gold car," she said bluntly.

"Thanks, you just might have that A++ you was talking about."

"Hey, I done told you, I got the goods. Where we headed? I didn't mind getting up helping you out, cause' you've had a rough weekend."

"I need you to ride me past an associates of mines house. I need to pick something up from him," I said, grinning to myself. The Diamond King was playing on the radio.

"Turn it up," she motioned as we thought the same thing. "R.I.P," she said as the bass drowned out the last of her words. Her G-Wagon was clean. Usually women are too busy to have their cars looking good in the inside, but hers looks freshly detailed.

"How do you keep your car so clean," I said while slowly turning the music down."

"Hey, what you doing? That's my song. The Making of a Diamond King, my diamonds bling, my diamonds fling. Sumtin sumtin sumtin sumtin."

"You don't even know all of the words," I told her.

She giggled, "I'm trying, but you messing with my music. This song came out at midnight. He already has over 20 million views on YouTube in less than 8 hours. Niggas hating. They didn't want to see that man reign. That's why they killed him."

"Who details your car?" I asked.

"Oh, I get it done down at Big Flea shop. You know the guy that used to work for Turtle before getting his own thing poppin."

"I probably know him by face. His name doesn't ring a bell."

"Well, he does know what he doing. He offers fleet deals. You know you got all of them cars. I'm sure he will give you that family discount. Tell him I sent you," she offered.

"I got someone already, but usually female's cars aren't this clean. That's why I asked."

"I keep my car clean baby. Growing up around just brothers I learned a thing a two about cars. I can change a flat and I used to get under the hood a little bit. Nothing heavy, but enough to diagnose minor issues. My daddy and 'em kept me on my toes."

"That's what's up. Make a right at the next street and park. I will get out and walk down."

I grabbed an old cloth grocery bag that had a hole in the corner of it off the seat behind me and placed the corner with the hole over the barrel of my pistol. I wrapped the handles around my arm tight enough, so the bag won't move easily, but loose enough that my slide can move freely.

"What you up to Craft? I ain't finna be an accessory to nothing. No co-dee or nothing. I'm gonna point yo' ass out in court. That man right there MR. PROSECUTOR!"

"Oh, girl. Shut up. Quit being so loud," I whispered.

"You know I was just playing. You're cranky as hell. I know it ain't, cause' you need some pussy cause you stay fucking."

I closed the door ignoring her last rant as I crossed the street heading to the first house on the left. The modest red brick house with the loose third step almost took me out the last time I was here. The wooden screen door with cheap brown paint swung back and forth in the slight breeze. It was eerie like a scary movie, but in this flick I'm the Boogieman. I slid in between the two doors timing it as the brown one opened once again in the wind. I grabbed the tarnished knob firmly. I began to twist it. Something told me to look at Angie. She wasn't paying any attention, too busy with her interior light on looking for something. I tried to motion her to cut it off, but it did no good. I pushed the door as someone pulled the door. I crashed to the floor hitting my knee hard on the threshold as I caught my fall with my gun in hand.

"Damn, that hurt!" The wind was on the other side of the door. The house was empty except for a few miscellaneous things that wasn't of much importance. All of the usual hiding places were my targets. I checked everything trying to get a clue. Behind the fridge and in the drawers. Nothing so far, I even checked under the couch to name a few. The wooden floor crept with every step I made. "This nigga make enough money to get some shit fixed around here," I said to the shack of a house. In the bathroom, there was a picture of Ice and I standing by the window. My arms were wrapped around her. The picture was taken from a distance. I remember it clearly, because that's when I was telling her about my vision for the building. "What this nigga been doing? Stalking her or something. He's a real weirdo. How he goin' out like this talking all that righteous pro black shit while trying to take out my queen."

On the back of the picture there was something written in Ice's handwriting, but I couldn't tell what her chicken scratch said. Why would Ice write on the back of a picture of us that she didn't take. Folding the picture up, I put it in my left back pocket and headed out of the empty house. The unmistakable sound of tires screeched as cars pulled up. I hurried to the back window hoping the loud ass floor don't give me away. Unmarked police cars pulled up to my location. "I don't need this type of shit right now." I guess Ira's big black ass was very popular this morning. I exited through the cut in the back fence that he didn't get fixed either, and made my way to an alley that would lead me away from the street. I would be able to sneak up on Angie from behind. Shid, I don't know if she called, a neighbor called, or what. Few minutes and a light jog later, I got to Angie. She was hiding with her seat all the way back. I knocked on the window three times. That was out of habit, I guess.

"Angie, open up the door!" I commanded.

"Craft, is that you?"

"Girl, open this damn door!" I spoke in an urgent whisper. I hopped in as soon as the doors clicked to view the police from a distance. My eyes are not as good as they used to be, but I could make out the murder squad detective by his walk.

"I told you; I am not about this life. I'm ready to go," she demanded.

"Girl, chill out."

"I was so scared. I didn't want to leave you, but I did think about it. I'm just saying," she admitted.

"I thought you might have called them or something. I saw you playing with your interior light looking for something. Next thing I know, they pulled up."

"You crazy. I was looking for my lip gloss. My lips was feeling dry. They poppin now ain't they?" I gave her that IDAF look. "I get to talking a lot when I'm nervous. My bad," Angie disclosed.

"I need you to relax and focus," I said, redirecting her attention. "If they see us, it's gonna be a shootout fo sho!"

"I'm on my Dead Prez shit. I got a strap to help out," she revealed reaching under the compartment by her steering wheel and pulled out a hot pink compact 40-caliber pistol. "I don't play all of the time. Turtle bought this for me. He said I needed protection."

I'm not much of a praying man, but I hope to God, they don't see us. I can't watch them and watch her too. As the murder squad's business concluded, I wondered what they wanted with Ira. I'm sure it wasn't about Ice unless him and Tags were working together, and somehow his name came up.

"Angie, you be in everybody's business. Do me a favor."

"You ain't gonna keep on throwing shade. What you need?" she asked with an attitude.

"Can you look up somebody's record to see what they went to jail for?"

"Yeah. Me and my home girls use this one website all the time, before we go out on any dates, cause' dudes is crazy nowadays," she said.

"Look up Ira Manafort for me."

"Big I, that's who you're looking for? He be on that odd shit. He talk all that queen this and queen that, and will fuck around and hold you hostage. They said he went to jail for manslaughter when he was younger. He killed a man for sleeping with the girl that he used to have feelings for, had a baby by, or something."

"Could you look him up for me?" I repeated, scolding her.

"Yessa Boss," she said sarcastically.

"Your ass always playing."

"You just being too serious. You need to lighten up."

"My circumstances don't call for me to lighten up, but to step my game up. Shid, I've been taking things way too light."

"I'm just messing with you. But on the real, I'mma need more than a XL plate from Big Barb's," greedy said. Looking out of the rearview mirror was a habit I learned the hard way. Twenty minutes later, Ice's truck drove past us and into what looked like the alley's entrance.

"Wait right here. I'll be right back! This time call or text me if them folks pull up. Don't leave without warning me with your tough talking, scary ass."

"My bad. I'm just a little rusty that's all," she said, lying through her teeth. I proceeded to find Ira "Big I" Manafort with my murder bag in tow.

Chapter 12

The unique custom, pink truck pulled two houses up from Ira's residence. I blended with the background like a lion in the wild waiting for their prey to appear. The brake lights were on. The truck was in park. Then the door opened and out appeared a woman in an orange Hijab getting out of the passenger side. I was unable to see her face, but the man on the driver's side was the man of the hour, Big I, who wore a camouflage jacket like the one my uncle had. He had a slight limp that was revealed when he pulled a child from the back seat. I waited until he had the child firmly in his arms before I approached. That big nigga already got a body, so he ain't getting no fare ones. I stalked at a fast pace not trying to blend, not trying to hide, and my gun was aimed at his head. Getting loser with every step. The woman in the orange garb's back was turned with her key out ready to enter the door. I approached them with deadly intent. Aiming the gun at her, I forced him to freeze. He wouldn't sacrifice the queen to protect the king. He paused like a big statue in the woods, shocked that I had the drop on him.

"Don't you dare scream. I will splatter your shit all over that wall."

"Please don't hurt my baby," she murmured.

"I'm not here to hurt you, or the baby. My beef is with him," I said, motioning her to get away from the door. Big I looked at me without fear, but he was leery of my next move.

"Get over there NOW! No right there! Don't be trying no cute shit. Big I, you are a hard guy to find. You know why I'm here. You did some fuck shit that you know wasn't called for," I became excited, confronting him.

"Fuck you, nigga!" speaking his final line before he exited stage left. "I ain't no king today, brother. Huh? Say fuck you king!" His eyes bulging now as his nervousness started to set in. "I said say it," I spoke with the calm of an executioner.

"Man, just go ahead and kill me then!" Big I insisted.

"Aight den tough nigga!" I yelled.

"Wait! My baby! Please don't hurt my baby!" the lady reasoned. The toddler looked to be 3 or 4, still sleeping in his arms during all the commotion.

"Walk to him slowly. You give her the baby. Any funny shit, I'm shooting both of yawl asses," I said coldly. He tossed her the baby and ran for it nearly knocking me down. I regained my balance and let off two shots. One hit him in the back of his leg and exiting out of his shin. He crumbled immediately.

"Aw shit! You shot me in my leg man. Goddammit! This shit burns like a muthafucka!" he held on to his leg as if it was going to cease the pain that had just begun.

"Why you do that to Ice? She didn't deserve that."

"Nigga, you shot me over a bitch. I thought this was about some other shit," he spoke faintly with teary, bloodshot eyes.

"The murder squad looking for you already about that other shit. Don't worry, today is your last day. You got mad at Ice 'cause she was feeling me, and she didn't want you. What type of weak shit is that!" I wondered shaking my head in disgust.

"That bitch loved your dirty ass draws. It was many days I consoled her when you was out being the nigga that you are. Good morning text. Bringing her lunch. Opening the doors for her. All that chivalrous shit, but she was in love with you."

"She still is in love with me. You hurt her body, but her soul is still strong. Her heart still beats for me, weak ass nigga!"

"I came over there to check on her after she was late Saturday. She was floating. All happy and shit. Talking about you just left. The smell of sex and breakfast all in the air. The couch was covered with her plush Michigan blanket. I just wanted to see what she was hiding that's all. She grabbed my arm to prevent me, and I just snapped. My big hand came slamming against her face, finally getting her to submit to my will. I didn't mean to, but once I started, it felt so good to relieve myself of years of frustration and rejection from her. All the love that I had for her, she spit in in my face fucking with you," the hater paused to spit in the middle of his confession.

He wiped his mouth. "All of them women you had. All of the times I cheered her up when she felt like you made her feel invisible."

Whack! "Who the fuck you do you think you are?" I demanded after hitting him in the head. I knew he was seeing stars with all that astrological shit he be talking. Whack! Whack! The gun came crashing down on the side of his face continuously. I opened his head up in the process. He held his face, but those mitten size hands couldn't prevent the flow of blood as it made its way between his fingers, splashed on his camouflage jacket, and onto the rundown pavement in the alley.

"Ain't nobody worrying about dying nigga. Just don't hurt my sister," he begged as he bowed. She stood there in semi-shock holding the baby close preventing the child from hearing justice being served. Her eyes big and round were covered partially by her hijab. She didn't feel sorrow for the man lying injured on the ground too proud to beg for his life, or wise enough to know that it wouldn't make any difference. Whack! Another blow. This time to the bridge of his nose. He screamed wakening the baby. The mother held the child even tighter.

But the voice was too familiar to the child's ears to resist, "Mommy what's wrong with my daddy? I want my daddy!" the child continued. By the face, I could finally see it was a boy.

"Ira it looks like you have a problem,"....my soliloquy interrupted by a call from Angie. Usually, I would just ignore it, but my temporary side kick may have some news.

"Make it quick baby?" I said, rushing the flow.

"Them guys from earlier are coming down the street headed to the front of the house. I don't know if some more are coming down the alley, but it looks like your time is up," Angie warned.

"Shit!" I motioned the lady and "little I" into the house. I put the gun to his head. "Nigga the only reason I ain't gonna pull the trigger is cause the murder squad is here for you. I'm not going to harm your child or that woman. They ask what happened, tell them you got robbed and go wherever they want you to go. Say your prayers or whatever cause' it's lights out," I promised.

The look in his eye of a pawn... defeated. We hurried inside the same door that she left cracked enough to slide in.

"Thank you for saving my child. I don't know what has gotten into him lately," she confessed, unsuccessfully trying hold back her tears.

"He woke me up out of my sleep saying someone was out to get him, and they already hurt Shanice," she sobbed.

"He hurt her. The only reason I didn't kill that man is because your son was woke. There are some men here to get him for something that is unrelated to this situation. It seems he stole something from the cartel that they want repaid in blood."

"I don't know what to do," her voice saddened.

"Right now, just listen. We can't afford to be noticed. Take" little I" into the bathroom. Close the door and get into the tub. Tell him to be very quiet. There he is!" a voice yelled. There was commotion in the alley. One of the soldiers from the other side of the window pointed a gun. Another car with government tags screeched up. I knew this shit was official and the murder squad was untouchables.

Chapter 13

"Leave him for me!" a soft-spoken authoritarian voice rang through the window. It was none other than Det. Corral dressed in another suit: dark colored maybe blue or black. He held a cane made of hard wood that made him appear to be more like a shepherd than a detective. I knew it was going to be a crucifixion. No questions asked, he raised the wooden staff to the heavens and came down like thunder. WHACK! The giant nearly reduced to mash with one blow. He paced around in a circle. Experience told me he wasn't finished.

He was thinking like my daddy used to before he continued. WHACK! "I don't know why they let yawl niggas think yawl was kings! You muthafuckas started thinking yawl was gods. They sent me, the god killer to clean up this fucking mess." WHACK! "I hate the site of you niggas. Loud music playing. Pants hanging off of your asses and making it hard for the rest of us." WHACK! WHACK! Brutal blow after brutal blow, I couldn't turn away even though I almost threw up.

The color struck man bludgeon Ira like a slave trying to get a butter biscuit. He was lifeless after a few strikes. The force of the cane ripped his face into pieces caving in the top of his head. Finally, it removed his mask. Maskless. Lifeless. His fatigue jacket covered with blood and brain matter like a suicidal soldier taking his own life. Still the blows didn't stop. Whatever the message was it got across. The back alley was the perfect location to dispose of someone. I was the only eyewitness and I ain't see shit. Backing out of the window unnoticed, I headed to the bathroom to check on his next of kin.

I shook my head to the mother to signal it was done. Teary-eyed and weak, she grabbed my hand. I helped her out of the tub. The child was unaware, playing with a small car that he probably would play with during bathtime. Ira had to go. He violated too many rules and hurt too many people. I felt a certain way about his son growing up without him, but it is what it is. Inside the bathroom mirror, there were several pictures of Ice and a few more with us together. I even saw a picture of Church outside of his hotel with the girl from the party. Ira the cameraman gave all the info to Tags. I would take a picture of his lifeless body, but what was left of him was taken by his killers.

"He told me he was doing some private investigative work for his friend, trying to protect

Ice from her no-good man." Judging me with her eyes calling me no good every step of the way. "He hid something in the trashcan under the garbage bag, because he said no one would check there." She walked over to the white garbage can in the kitchen and lifted the bag with just pieces of torn mail in it. Underneath was the treasure buried in a black plastic bag wrapped in several layers of tape.

"He told me where these were in case of an emergency."

I grabbed a knife out of the drawer. I carefully cut into the gift-wrapped present with no name, revealing the forged documents that Tags used to steal those cars. Creating a chain reaction, it left bodies scattered around town. I could use these as leverage if the murder squad needed to be bargained with. I thanked the recently widowed woman for the gift. It revealed in detail how he was able to get the cars. It was a signature on a few of the sheets that looked familiar, but the name didn't match. A signature that I have seen on plenty of business documents. My good buddy Dick, or Richard LePhantom as these documents suggest. At this point, nothing shocked me. I already knew I couldn't trust anybody, so that's how I was going to play my hand. Balls deep and all in.

"You need to get as far away from here as possible. That pink jeep was reported stolen, so you can't drive that. If you have a vehicle or a way to get out of town, do so immediately. Those people that Ira fucked over are very dangerous."

"We can go over my sister's house; she lives in Alabama." One of the most beautiful skies I ever laid my eyes on was in Bessemer, Alabama, I reminisced. Stormy and I visited her relatives there, but I caught myself before my mind drifted.

"Do you need a ride somewhere?" I asked. "No, thank you. We will be fine. I just need to gather a few items before I leave," she replied.

I waited patiently communicating with Angie through text messages making sure the coast was clear before I came out and hit the streets. I didn't know if they recovered what they were looking for, but they got rid of one of the pieces for me. The enemy of my enemy is my friend, indeed. Finally, the coast was clear, and things were looking up. My phone was charging in Angie's truck as I thought about my next move. Tags will be dealt with. I got to get to him before the murder squad does. The result will be the same, that is for sure. But my personal touch will one up the murder detective. My lawyer was gonna get his shit peeled too, since it seems he was a part of this whole thing from the beginning. It was Monday morning, a quarter till noon, and Isis just crossed my mind. I needed to check her temperature, cause' she didn't even call about my house burning down to make sure I was cool.

"Hey Angie. Look up the local news on your phone to see if there is any information about the fire at my building, or about Church's murder." Shit quiet and that's not like the streets not to be talking. Gotta hit Unc up, but I'm sure he should know about this by now. Maybe, he just waiting on me to bring it to his attention. I ain't looking forward to speaking with him, but my hand was a lot better than it was 24 hrs. ago. Before the end of this week, I will be looking for this business to be concluded and my reign to be solidified.

"Nothing about Church is in the news at least not yet," Angie reported.

"Damn! A nigga gets his head cut off and he still don't make the news. That shit deep," I said, taking a quick look up to the sky as if I could see my friend's face in the clouds.

"I hate to hear Church died like that. That shit is so…."

"I don't even want to talk about it no more," I interrupted, preventing myself from thinking about the situation too hard.

"Dang, you just cut me off," she said in an irritated tone.

"What did they say about the fire?" I ignored her getting the conversation back on track.

"The fire is still under investigation. They say it looks like arson."

"Shit, I know it had to be. Somebody set my shit ablaze."

"You smelling a lil' musty over there, boss. You want me to run you over to my house so you can freshen up?" she asked wanting to insist it.

I gave my arms a sniff. My deodorant had broken up with me. So much for the 48-hr. protection they advertised. "Naw, take me to my place on the west side to freshen up. I can look over some things in Ice's apartment first and get the most out of these musty ass clothes before changing," I said, leaning the seat back with my arms up just so I could share the wealth.

"Put your arms down! You stank!"

"To the west, driver. To the west, I say!" I said, ignoring her request. She busted a U through the stop sign. Blasting the music, as if to drown out my funk, as she headed to my last place of refuge.

Chapter 14

Once at the building, I had Angie drop me off. She wanted to help me some more, but I just told her to keep me abreast with anything regarding Church or the fire at the house. I figured someone would be in touch with me for questioning regarding the fire, but no one as of yet. If it wasn't for the murder squad, I might have a fair shot. I kind of wanted to be alone. This whole building was like our place together even though we lived separately. I didn't entertain anyone here out of respect for her. Knowing how deeply she felt for me, I tried to be mindful of that.

Cutting through the crime scene tape, I entered the labyrinth. Ice's place had a dank smell to it; the food on the dishes started to turn into something else. The wind chimes were still. I cracked the windows to let the air circulate and get the vibrations up. Removing everything from the safe was my second priority. Then into her bedroom. The footprints on the vanilla carpet were from the different investigators, I'm sure. She was very orderly, but free, if that makes any sense. She wasn't as rigid as I am. Her energy flowed freely. Feng Shui is what it's called. I think she said it was Japanese.

"You're always so wound up. You need to relax sometimes."

"I can't afford to relax. I have things I need to get accomplished. I'm trying to build an empire."

"At what cost," she asked not expecting an answer.

"At all costs," I replied quickly. Probably just bravado on my part a little, but I meant every word. Coming up, finances were the solution to all our problems. Evictions and repossessions made me want to own everything. I didn't want to relive certain shit again.

"You're holding onto the past too much," she revealed.

"My scars have scabs, but I still feel the cuts as if they are happening right now," I confided.

"Baby, I ain't saying you don't still hurt, or that the pain will stop one day. I want you to stop masking things with material stuff when your spirit is what needs to be healed."

"Praise the lawd," I would say. "I'z been healed," I joked to change the subject.

"You don't take nothing serious. I'm not joking with you. Look into that mirror and see yourself for who you are, and not who people want you to be, or need you to be for them. Look into that mirror, and find who you need to be for you," she pleaded.

"That's enough preaching for the day." Her words were true and sometimes poetic, but I knew they came from a place I wasn't meant to listen to and occupy at the same time. I opened the curtains to allow the sunshine to cleanse the darkness. Opening her bedroom window had always been a task for some reason. The window comes off track when you lift it. I was supposed to have that fixed weeks ago.

Once I rigged the window to stay open, the air just flowed in like peace riding on a wave. The picture of Ice and her mother that she kept on her dresser was always a favorite of mines. It was a time before she ever had to consider pawning her innocence or fighting just to breathe the very fresh air that she coveted so much. It was a time long before I met the woman in the picture for the first time. Her partial smile couldn't cover up the hurt that she felt from the man holding the camera taking the picture. The one that she wanted to be her savior and remove all that was bad from her world.

Mrs. Mitchell was a sweet lady at times, but she never forgave her husband for moving on. The bitterness permeated into the way she raised

Shanice to harbor resentment towards her father. The daughter's bitterness began to match the mother's. He paid his child support, but Mrs. Mitchell never really wanted him to be a part of her life. Shanice would later reveal that her mother was angry at her father, because he changed his life for the better when he met his new wife. I guess he became the savior to the new woman and that fact offered her mother no salvation. Sometimes people just want you at your best when they can directly benefit from it, or control the benefits you get from it. I placed the old silver picture frame down and immediately picked up her perfume that I purchased for her birthday last year. I love how it smelled on her skin. The way she placed a touch of it behind her ears and on her wrists, so the scent flew in the air like a field of fresh flowers.

"It irks me when people put on too much perfume. All it takes is just a touch," she would say as she got prepared for the evening. I traced the handprints on the mirror with my finger from round two on Saturday. Smeared, but still clear enough to recall that special moment when barriers were broken, and anxieties were freed. Those anxieties have since been destroyed and replaced by different challenges with varying degrees of difficulty. I can't wait until this is all over, so I can hold her again. Smell that scent of that natural shampoo that she loves so much. The smell of that thick lotion that she likes, but I don't, cause' it takes too long to rub into your skin.

I came here looking for answers, clues, or something that will help me understand the madness that has taken place. Her beautiful soul was strapped down and forced fed through tubes while awaiting the time to be reconnected to this world. There was nothing of any significance in Ice's place. It was time to freshen up and get moving. There were plenty of questions that still needed to be answered. I paused outside of her door momentarily to gather myself and catch my breath.

Losing her would be losing someone special and genuine. A piece of me would be underdeveloped and buried before being able to cherish it.

Chapter 15

Upstairs was a world that was different from the world that my best friend replicated in her loft. My colors are dark and cold from wall to wall with high tech appliances. However, it is absent the warm, welcome home feeling I get when going to the floor underneath me. A few pictures are on my walls, but no plants, no cages or aquariums. I am the only sign of life, marooned on an island of my creation. At times, it's the reason I stay and other times the reason I leave. My open windows are the only thing that is similar. We both love the way the air brings freshness.

At my place, we would do all the movies, video games, but anything that didn't require gadgets, we would do downstairs at the low-tech retreat. Board games that we both loved. I even let her borrow my chessboard. A piece from that board scarred Tag's bitch ass and possibly saved her life. The note that Stormy left I half read, along with the money, laid crumpled on the floor. She even had the nerve to put lipstick kisses on it. I grabbed the letter to read her propaganda.

Dear Jont'e,

I'm sorry I caused all this confusion. I was crying out for some love and attention from you. We had the material things, but we lost track of the little things: the walks in the parks, the long talks on the phone, and the dinner dates. What happened to honesty, huh?

My time with you seemed to be so broken up, because you always had other obligations that you needed to take care of. I feel that you put everything before me, so what was I supposed to do but take something you love more than me. I took the money and look how long it took you to miss it. Even when I'm trying to divert your attention, so I can have some of it, you still don't find out until it is too late. I'm tired of this life. You will always love me how you love me, and that will always be partially divided into the other things professionally and personally that you love more than me. Even that green Buick got more attention than me. That's why I flattened them fuckin' tires.

Tonight, I celebrate in fire. I lay myself on the altar as a sacrifice to the gods. I'm going to burn your fucking heaven to the ground. I want you to remember that you created this side of me.

Yeah, I have another copy of your key.

If you love me, you will save me from myself.

If not, FUCK IT!

Forever Always;
77

Stormy always had to try and get one up on me. I stewed in my clothes full of soiled dirt, sweat, blood, and who knows what else. She always had to get the last laugh, the last word, and depending on how hungry she was, the last slice of pizza.

"If you love me, you wouldn't mind giving me your last," she would say.

"If you loved me, you wouldn't even ask for my last," would be my reply.

"Yeah, but if I'm asking for your last, that means I really need it."

"Well hell, if I give you my last, what the fuck I'm gonna have?"

"You're an enterprising man. Your last will never be your last," she responded quickly while beating me to the last slice of pizza. The middle piece with all the toppings and cheese that I would usually get first. Her big bites left me just the corner. She would place it on my tongue. I would gulp it up like a doggy treat.

"See, I told you your last wasn't your last."

I called Stormy's number just to see if she was just writing this letter for attention. No answer. It just kept ringing. After several redial attempts, I knew I had to prepare for the day no matter the outcome. I jumped off the couch ready to wash every inch of the funk off me. The clothes were sticky even though cool air was flowing through my window. Showers always made my day better. The more complicated the day, the longer the shower.

Today, it's gonna be at least 30 minutes. No music, just concentration. My heart is in a vengeful place. I'm not even going to ask for forgiveness. We aren't meant to be forgiven for some things anyway. The hot water came crashing down massaging my aching muscles, opening my clogged pores, relieving me of my pains and numbing me of my reality. My scarred hands were up against the wall showing only a fraction of what my last couple of days had been like.

"I want the strength and wisdom to destroy my enemies far and wide. Never allowing them to regain strength, consciousness or life. Destroyed with the rest of those who came for my head. AMEN," I said then lifted my head again.

Tears flowed, even though I didn't want to feel that part of life. That part where the losses are significant enough to make you pause. A chain of events marred by decisions I have made, that have led up to this day. A day of loss and a day of extreme revelation. I am very thankful for both.

While taking deep breaths of air and plotting to take the breath of those that remain, I answered to hear, "Why didn't you answer your phone. I know you seen my texts."

"I was in the shower. What news do you have for me Angie?" I asked, annoyed.

"This tea is hot as hell and I gots to spill it. When you hear this, you're gonna be shocked. Let me see how I can put this."

"Damn, Angie. Spill it already!" I hurried her.

"Your funky ass is so impatient."

"I'm back to fresh now," I joked to keep her from getting angry at my impatience.

"You needed it," Angie replied.

"Girl, what is it?"

"Ok, they found a body in your place. It's not official yet, but I know somebody who is close with the case," she revealed.

"Is it male or female?" I asked.

"It's a male for your information, but that's none of your business."

"The body is in my house! Girl, damn! Quit playing!"

"Oh, that body is burned to a crisp. They can't tell if it is male or female right now. They need to run some tests. This some forensic files shit!"

"They must have to check the dental records or something," I thought out loud.

"I'm already on my way to pick you up. I figured you would need me again. Even if you don't want to admit it. You know you a prideful ass nigga. Folks shooting atcha, burning down your house, taking ya money, and you still want to do it all by yourself," Angie said, reliving event after event.

"Girl, just bring your talky ass on if you coming," I commanded.

"You know I'm right though." I hung up the phone, understanding that the only thing left was to go right even if I'm wrong. I couldn't stand still allowing the walls to collapse on me. Thissa' all hands-on deck situation. I called Dick, but there was no answer. I didn't leave a message. It was just to let him know that I knew about him scheming and stealing inventory from the docks. Shona changed her cellphone number all together. Her receptionist said she called in sick for the whole week. She ran with her guilty ass. I may have to give her momma another visit and some convincing. I tucked the letter in my back-pants pocket and placed the forms from Ira's house out in front of me. I went through each sheet individually trying to see if it was something I overlooked earlier. Invoices, bills of lading, everything looked official even down to the watermarks and the notary seals.

Tags double skept ass knew what he was doing with these forgeries. Paperwork alone isn't going to get him access to the merchandise. There must be an inside man who could help get him in contact with the right people. Even the ability to move cars on that scale would take more than him, Ira, and Dick. Somebody had to move the cars to another location.

I needed to make a few calls with the burner phone to see if I could ruffle some feathers and shake some shit loose.

Chapter 16

Stepping out into the early afternoon air was better than being in my place locked away from the world, at least for the moment. "Why are you out here blowing your horn? You could have texted me," I replied a bit irritated.

"I'm sorry, Lil' Stanky. I'm so used to doing that when I'm picking up my girls when we are getting ready for the turn up," she said, joking as usual.

"This ain't no turn up mission. You might have to use that pretty ass pistol," I said seriously.

"I ain't scared to clear the crowd. Doesn't my outfit scream secret mission, double agent?"

"How black yoga pants scream secret mission with all that ass back there?"

"You always got your mind in the gutter. It's all natural too," she replied more with her movements than her words.

"I know I saw a needle mark when I was putting a passion mark on your booty," I smiled.

"Boy, stop it! This been here basically all my life. Now, it's just chiseled in all the right places."

"It looks a lot better since I chiseled on it the other day," I admitted.

"That dick is just decent. I'mma give you a D+."

"Lookin' mafucka!" was the only reply for the chiseled booty double agent trying to steal my lingo! "Any word from your source regarding the body?" I asked.

"No, he hasn't called me back yet," Angie said with confidence. That body could belong to anyone even possibly Stormy.

Somewhere deep down I hoped it wasn't, even though I wished it was as I thought to myself.

"I don't think Stormy's that crazy. She has issues but mostly that shit came from fucking with you," she lectured.

"The fuck you mean… fucking with me. I'm a good man."

"Yeah, you are a good man in a world full of bad ones. Don't get me wrong, I know you gonna hold your lady down, make sure she is fly, but you ain't never gonna give your all to a relationship. I don't know if it's commitment issues or trust issues. Hell, it's probably both."

"Don't be trying to diagnose me. I give a healthy dose of myself when it comes to relationships. Women just want men to fall in love as if love ain't enough by itself," I insisted.

With a look on her face like I had said something about her momma, "What's wrong with falling in love?"

"Nothing, if it works for you. I just prefer to stand in love," I explained.

"You always play on words. What's the difference?" she asked.

"The bottom line is if you have communication, respect, trust, honesty and love, your relationship should foster beautiful memories even if it doesn't last forever," I elaborated.

"I'm not even looking for forever any longer. It's hard enough to get repeat dates," she said, laughing out loud.

"Yeah, it's probably because of your driving," I explained while double checking my seatbelt.

After riding around following dead end leads, I received a call from the police department wanting to question me about the body that they found but have yet to identify. I handed Angie the letter Stormy wrote full of threats that predicted a fire at my penthouse.

"Damn! You said she was crazy. I hope she ain't mess around and kill herself over your ass," she responded letter in hand.

"Why you think it's because of me?"

113

"I hope she ain't kill herself period is what I meant to say," she recanted.

"Setting a fire like that, I'm glad only one person got killed. Hopefully, it was the person who torched my place," I said honestly.

"What if it was her? Do you still feel that way?"

"Hell yeah! Like I said, more than one person could have died who had nothing to do with this."

"I don't know about that, but I guess if you play a stupid game, you win stupid prizes," Angie countered going against the grain. "What are you going to say to the police?"

"The truth. That I don't know shit," I insisted.

"What about that letter? Aren't you going to give it to them?"

"I might pull it out, if they are trying to blame me for the shit, but other than that I'm keeping it close. Angie, while I'm here clearing my name, contact the officer on the inside, see what he knows."

"You don't want a lawyer before you talk to them peoples?" she whispered.

"That's a different card. I will play it, if need be. Also, I have an alibi for the fire, so it ain't like I'm guilty," I protested.

"You know damn well it ain't about innocence or guilt. It's about which one you can prove."

"Ok Law and Order, chill with all this interrogating you doing."

Chapter 17

I walked into the massive building at a casual pace. They already viewed me as a suspect, and their hands were on their pistols as they greeted me. There were no signs of the murder squad, so I felt less anxious, and more relaxed like this was just standard procedure.

"I received a call about my penthouse being torched. I told them when I was available that I would be down here to speak to someone."

"Your name sir?" he asked.

"Craft," I answered as he avoided eye contact.

"Is that with a K or a C?" he questioned.

"Craft. C-R-A-F-T," I disclosed. I get the spelling my name thing from my grandma. She would always say period at the end of any word like she was notifying the spelling bee judges that her word was complete.

"Thank you, sir. You can have a seat. Someone will be with you momentarily," he instructed.

I took a seat in one of the many chairs covered in hard black plastic that were placed uniformly up against the wall squeezing the rest of the freedom out of you. They were the four-play before the accusations started. Before the procedural questions became hostile.

"Good evening, Craft is it?" I heard as I sat with my head down flipping through a National Geographic Magazine. I knew the voice instantly. I could see Italian loafers in black that looked freshly wiped with a spot intentionally missed just so he could have a souvenir of the man he beat to death. A small piece of what looked like brain matter stuck to the left toe of his otherwise meticulous shoes. I raised my head slowly looking at that devil in the eye.

"Detective Corral, is it?" I replied. He extended his hand for me to shake it, and it instantly became a game of strength. His grip tightened as my grip tightened. I wasn't going to let him play me like a bitch. Our eyes locked speaking a language of death as the detective released his grip, and I followed at a slower pace to give him something to think about.

"I need to have a word with you" he said, rubbing his right hand as he spoke. "Mr. Craft, it seems like your name keeps coming up in my investigation."

"That's bullshit, I ain't did nothing!"

"Lower your voice, sir. There isn't a need to elevate your tone. This is off the record. Look at it as a courtesy," he said with such arrogance and contempt. I wanted to permanently remove that smug ass smirk from his face. He continued, "I heard you was down here about that little fire at your penthouse. The rumor is that one of your business associates' body was in that fire. I think I may know who it is, but I have to wait like everyone else to get the results."

"You dirty muthafucka!" I yelled.

"Mind your manners before I take over the procedural questioning and turn it into something a little less procedural and a lot more punishing," he threatened.

"Nigga, I ain't worried about shit you saying."

"Nigga this, nigga that. I kill niggas for the fun of it." He looked down at his shoes and grinned slyly, "Craft I will be seeing you again. You know I don't mind making house calls."

I can't stand that Uncle Tom ass nigga. He hates himself and anything that reminds him of who he really is. Behind the badge and in that mirror reveals the face under the mask. That must be a horrible life looking at yourself in the mirror and hating what you see, because it doesn't match who you believe you are.

"I see you have met Detective Corral. He is one of our finest officers," was the greeting from the detective planning to accuse me of arson and possibly murder. He wore a white dress shirt, a necktie with green and blues meshed in a paisley-like design. His pants looked as if they had stains, old and new, not meticulous like the murder detective. He was probably less than 10 years in, because he seemed as if he was offering hope with his presence, but he still turned a blind eye to the same corruption that those lesbian groups march about. "Follow me down the hall, Mr. Craft. I'm glad you can make it down. No need to worry, the questions are fairly routine at this point. The fire was considered to be arson, but we don't know if the person whose remains were recovered was the person who started the fire or not."

After the session of routine questioning came to an end, it was about an hour or so later. He wasn't really sounding like he suspected me. I gave him my whereabouts and told him I would cooperate fully and that was basically it. I was expecting pictures of the charred remains like on T.V. or a board with my picture at the top of the pyramid. The questioning was really basic.

He was trying to gage my responses and taking notes to look back on for the ah ha moment.

Chapter 18

"Hey Angie!" I greeted my sidekick; it was a relief to see her face.

"Well, what did they say? You got that look on your face like you was in there snitching."

"Leave the jokes up to me to tell. I'm funnier than you are anyway," I told her.

Hehehe! "You want to be the background singer and the lead. I have never ever seen anyone that wanted to do everything by themselves like you do. You don't always want to be alone like you pretend to be," my accuser spoke while I stepped up into her truck.

"If you gonna do all of this therapy work, at least let me lay down on that nice couch of yours."

"Why you hate hearing the truth? You only like the truth from your perspective. You don't want to see it coming towards you in the same loving way that you claim to send it out," she insisted.

"I ain't hardly afraid of the truth. Your version is more of an opinion. That's why I don't pay it much mind. I spoke to the head of the murder squad, and he knew something. He is playing his cards close to the chest as well," I revealed.

"What did he say?" Angie's itchy ears are always thirsty for the tea.

"To sum it up, the body is a business associate of mines. He still has a piece of Ira's brain matter he intentionally left on his shoe as a souvenir." He said, and I quote, "I don't mind killing niggas or making house calls."

"You better watch yourself. He sounds like a sick individual. He's probably a sociopath," she said, sounding very concerned.

"Whatever path he is, he better stay in his lane cause them split personality type niggas can get it. I got something for every personality."

"That was kinda funny Boo, but your delivery was off. You need to practice, your timing was off too," said my sidekick turned master instigator.

"Boo...I don't like that term," I replied.

"You don't like nothing but money, bitches and busting nuts," she giggled.

Ha! Ha! I couldn't hold back the laugh on that one. "That was pretty decent. I will let you tell a joke every now and then. You earned it baby."

"Speakin' of baby, do you ever think about having any of your own?" she asked.

"I used to think about it more often, but certain events have changed my mind. I live too fast for that now and I don't want to slow down at this point."

"Yeah, you do be zig zagging around."

"That sounds like I don't have a destination I know where I'm going," I proclaimed.

If your dick was as big as your ego, you wouldn't have the problems you're having right now."

"I'm big cock little cocky," I boasted.

You're back to not telling jokes cause that shit wasn't hardly funny," she laughed. She placed her soft hand on my left thigh and squeezed it gently, "I definitely feel the cocky, but the cock is hiding somewhere. Ha! Ha! Got'eem!" she cheered.

"I'm off of my A game today, cause' you're trying to let me have it with your knock knock jokes having ass."

"Boo, as in Boo it wasn't funny, not the one you don't like. See I do listen to you about your likes and dislikes. Damn, I'm hungry. Did you just hear my stomach growl. My stomach is touching my back," she greedily complained in between her punchlines. "It's your turn to treat," I reminded my hungry compadre who was speaking with her eyes like she does so well.

"All this driving I'm doing, I got my pistol locked and ready to blow like a hitter. I know you got me," she boasted.

"You dramatic as hell," I said.

"All of this backside; you know I keep an appetite."

"That ain't all that backside keeps an appetite for," I teased her.

"It keeps an appetite for that too, if I want it there. You know I gets it up and put it down."

"Yeah, it's definitely decent, if I do say so myself," I spoke with my eyes in a language that we didn't have time for. I really do it out of habit rather than necessity. "I know you don't want nothing but Big Barbs. Always the same place over and over," I complained.

"Yeah, I support the local black owned establishment that's been holding it down around the neighborhood since I was little. Everybody don't want snails and all that other shit you like to eat," she came back quickly.

"I don't eat no snails, but I like a variety of different foods," I admitted.

"Nigga you like a variety of everything especially women. Ramen noodles would be ok, if you could switch the spot, you parked your dick in every day."

"Now you went too far. I fucks with the noodles, but they got to be switched up too," I countered.

"What about the other part?" she asked.

"No comment, with your nosey ass. Order the food. I think I will go with the wings this time with that spicy strawberry sauce," I requested.

"Yeah, them do be bangin. I got you hip to them," she lied.

"Girl, please. Martha was still pretending to be faithful to your brother around the time I tasted them, and you know that was a minute ago."

"Ha-Ha-Ha!" We laughed in unison, because she is a married thotty.

"My brother loves her to death no matter what she does. I don't have nothing against her. She's just the female version of you," she said. If looks could kill Angie would be dead like her favorite rapper.

"Don't look at me like that. Oh no she didn't lookin' ass nigga. You be shooting that truth gun, but you keep a truth proof vest when it's fired back your way," she proclaimed.

"Order the food with your lying ass. I need to see what's up with the Bishop."

Chapter 19

"Bishop Blessings, have you heard from Shona? It is very important that I speak to her today," I urged.

"You sound like a collection agency," he said with sarcasm.

"Nigga, you know I'm lookin' to collect, so I guess I sound about right. Any word from her?" I hollered through the phone.

" Naw, I ain't heard from her, but I did hear about that fire at your palace in the sky. The Lord works in mysterious ways, don't he?" He said in a tone, as if I was supposed to learn my lesson, because my house burned down.

"The Lord, as you put it, is placing me in a position to understand certain mysteries. Do you want to be a part of the understanding, or the misunderstanding," I said.

"How can you sleep at night threatening a man of God?" Bishop asked.

"You ain't no more of a man of God than any man walking this earth. You prance around in flashy robes and take money from people, selling them something you have no proof exists," I revealed.

"Heaven is real!" the Bishop doubled down.

125

"It's not about it not being real, it's about you selling it."

"I'm a shepherd for the Lord's flock. I'm not selling anything. I'm collecting tithes like it say in the word…. Amen," he said self-righteously.

"Well, your tithe collecting ass better have Sister Evans, the younger or older one, to get in contact with me," I commanded.

"I haven't spoken to the elder sister Evans since I prayed for her hand that night. Hell, Shona ain't been to church since she got the hips and curves like her momma and started liking them boys. Cause she sho' did get it from her momma like that song say," the Bishop reminded me.

"Amen to that," I said. I can agree with the Bishop on that. I knew he probably used to bang Shona's momma with her old thieving ass.

The Bishop was worth more on the board than off right now. Where the fuck is Isis at? I still haven't heard from her. "Hey Angie, I just thought about something. Take me to Isis' art gallery. I haven't heard from her. I need to see what's up and where she stands with all of this."

"What's the address?" she requested.

"I'm not sure. Just Google, The Galleria."
She pulled into Big Barb's spot and it was packed. I should have asked Bishop what the special was

today, cause' it's packed like they selling them neck bones and potatoes. "Damn, it's packed today. I hope my order right, cause' you know I will take it back ASAP," Angie protested.

"You don't be putting hair in your own food, so you can get a free meal, do you? I joked.

"I'm not going to even dignify that with a response," she ignored.

Even though she tuned up her face with her hungry ass, she looked good in that all black. I always looked at Angie as someone cool almost like one of the fellas.

"Why you looking at me like that? You better eat those wings, cause' you ain't eating none of this. You working me today? I might need a massage," Angie suggested.

"I ain't looking at you like nothing. I'm just admiring your outfit. It looks good on you. I appreciate you helping me out, on some real shit," I admitted.

I stepped out of the truck to grab the food before she could even respond. At the pickup window, there was a young lady with a dark brown complexion, hair braided in an updo style and covered with a hair net. Her eyes, I noticed first, were hidden under her newly arched eyebrows. The color was greenish blue. I thought they were contacts, but after looking again, I could tell that they are real or some real good fakes.

"Good evening. May I have the name on the order?" Her voice was soft almost to a whisper, but the microphone to her mouth gave it the much-needed boost. She slid her cellphone to the side, so she can keep an eye on her notifications and the customers.

"John," I replied giving her my takeout alias.

"Order for John," she called back to the kitchen. "You like the Diamond King?" she asked out of the blue while grabbing my order."

"Yeah, he cool. Why what's up?" I inquired.

"He got this interview online talking about dying and different things like he predicted his death. He was so fine. The world is full of haters," she stated.

"Yeah, I know what you mean."

"Is that your wife in that truck waiting for you?" she pried looking back over my shoulder as she talked to me with her eyes. All she saw was dollar signs.

"Yeah, one of them," I said. She was cute, but that young girl couldn't afford me. You must be willing to get out of your comfort zone to be with me, and she looked too comfortable where she was at. I could feel her looking at me as I walked away, intrigued about me and my life. Probably just looking to be rescued.

"What was yawl talking about? She was staring hard when you was walking away," Angie said angrily.

"Nothing. She was talking about a video the Diamond King did online that seemed like he predicted his death."

"Oh, that's my baby with his fine ass! Me calling him fine don't make you retreat into your feelings does it? she questioned.

"Girl, please. Check your order before we pull off," I instructed.

"We should have eaten in. Don't spill nothing in my truck. I just got it detailed." The smell of the food was drowning out her instructions to not spill anything. The wings well done, and the sauce a shiny glaze that covered every inch.

"You know that southwest sauce is good on the fries. My home girl used to crave it when she was pregnant. Now it's something we do all the time," she gestured for me to open my mouth as she fed me a sample of her French-fried concoction.

"It's cool, but that ain't my thang," I said.

"You don't know what you're missing. Why you always get all flats when you ordering hot wings?"

"Because I like how my tongue goes in between the two little bones loosening the meat," I implied.

"Does everything have to be so sexual when it comes to you?" she responded.

"I'm not being sexual, but preferring flats is tied directly to my enjoyment of eating pussy."

"I guess the drums are for people who enjoy sucking dick then, huh?"

"Well I'mma just say any female that I have dealt with that enjoyed the drum part of the wing always pleasured me better orally," I revealed.

"Well, I like both."

"Don't you like both men and women anyway?"

"I do, but I don't. I prefer dick, but if I'm with a guy, I don't mind a little extra fun. I won't do a female by myself. I know it may sound strange, but I only like it when dick is involved," she confessed.

"Is that like semi bi, sike diking, or what?" I wondered.

"It ain't no title. It's just my personal preference."

Chapter 20

We devoured our food before even making it out of the parking lot with it. After she shared that one fry, it was every man for themselves. That spicy strawberry sauce was an award winner. Walking to the trash, I saw the young lady from behind the counter changing out the trash bag.

"Yawl ate that fast. Yawl must have been hungry," she questioned me. Getting a full look at her body, I noticed she was kinda curvy, not all the way, but she wasn't just a stick either. The red and yellow uniform fit real nice.

"Your uniform is super clean. You must do the least amount of work," I teased.

"I work, but I just work smart. I keep my clothes and my house clean. My momma would whoop our butts if we didn't have the house cleaned before she got home from work," she replied.

"That's what's up," I said in an uninterested tone.

"You remind me of someone, just an older version."

"Damn, is that a compliment or what?" I asked while sill being chill.

"I wasn't trying to insult you. You carry yourself like an important man. You're over the flash and the flossing stage. Now your money is making you money," she said intuitively.

"Is that what you see when you see me?" I asked, now more interested in the conversation.

"I see a leader, a man who can guide me in the right direction, who can direct me to be the best version of myself."

"You see all of that in just these few minutes?"

"How long should it take to see something real, if you know what real is?" She kinda turned me on, but I didn't take her number. I wasn't in the mood to play daddy or the retired Diamond King.

After getting the address, we headed to The Galleria, stomachs on full and feeling good.

"I told you; you can never lose that's my go to spot for family and friends when they come from out of town," Angie bragged.

"For the most part, I fucks with them. That spicy strawberry sauce is banging. I don't know who came up with it, but I definitely see it doing big thangs," I admitted.

"Them lips look like they like tasting out of the box flavors," she said.

"Turn that music up. I'mma take a short nap while you get us there in one piece," I said. The music on blast and it was none other than my ex-stepson giving his take on how to become a Diamond King. I will have to listen to this song one day just to see what he is talking about. R.I.P. Diamond King. I will see you in my dreams.

"Craft, wake up! You was snoring and talking in your sleep. I didn't know whether to take notes, or check if you were breathing. Who's the monster?"

"What you mean who is the monster?"

"The monster you was running from in your sleep?" she exposed.

"How you know I was running?"

"Because you seemed to be crying or something traumatic was going on. I was taught never wake a man abruptly out of their sleep. I pulled over when I thought about what my grandma told me."

Chapter 21

The area looked familiar. Once I wiped the sleep from my eyes, we had to be close to The Galleria. Kids were skateboarding, neon colors were in their hair, and piercings everywhere. This is the scene that Isis has influence over and gets influence from. Her rose grew defiantly from the concrete never turning back once fertile soil was available. The trees were well manicured, like an urban area with a suburban feel. Small eateries, microbreweries and gift shops surrounded the intimate size gallery that created such a buzz from online to her brick-and-mortar operation.

I called Isis' number while Angie tried to parallel park to see if there was any movement. The phone went to voicemail like someone pushed the button. I called from my burner phone and the results were the same. "Wait right here. I'll be right back," I said, hopping out and maneuvering around a parking meter making my way to the front door. The civilians that hurried through the streets had their faces buried in electronic devices, sunglasses on and used the latest ear buds. Their senses dulled while walking back and forth through this man-made maze. I pressed the buzzer with enough force to push it through the intercom.

Equipped with a camera that was for security and weeding out purposes, I'm sure.

"May I help you?" said a familiar nasally voice.

"Yes, this is Mr. Craft; here to see Isis," I responded like changing my voice could somehow change my face.

"I know who it is. I just want to know what you are doing showing your face here," said the woman of the hour.

"Isis open the door! What has gotten into you?"

"There is no reason I should open this door," she refused. I could sense her pouting through the intercom.

"Straighten up your face and open up!" I snapped.

"I will not. You know I needed you to do that show for me. You backed out at a time when I needed you," she explained.

"That was a business decision. Just open up. You can't take business personal," I assured her.

"I thought our friendship warranted something with a more personal touch. I am disappointed in you. I was looking forward to painting you in the raw flesh," she said.

"Open up this FUCKIN' door!" I commanded, no longer attempting to be patient.

"Dang, you ain't gotta curse at me."

As if my frustration was the magic phrase to open the door, first the buzz sounded, then I pulled the chrome covered door open. Instantly, she felt her passion overflowing into her work. She tirelessly hustled. Her innovation put her in the forefront of her profession. The pieces she sculpted were amazing. Even my old buddy Atlas was standing bold looking good while he held up the sky.

"Now Craft, how are you gonna come here unannounced like I didn't give you a favorable deal." She was dressed in clothes that were covered sporadically with clay, paint and whatever else she uses. Fingernails polished a beautiful green that I have never seen before. She positioned her hands, so I could see them without obstruction.

"Sorry to hear about your beautiful home being a total loss. Who body was it?" she asked placing her hands on her hips and tapping her feet as if she was somehow demanding the truth.

"Thanks for your concern. I don't have a clue of what or who it was," I said before pausing briefly. I watched as she bit her bottom lip with her Hollywood teeth; an uncontrollable habit of hers when she's in deep thought.

"This is a nice place you have here," I said.

"Thanks, but you've been here before," she reminded me.

"I don't remember. It must have been a long time ago."

"It wasn't that long ago," my want to be business partner countered.

"Refresh my memory!" I exclaimed.

"You remember you came to pick up the Atlas sculpture that I was going to have delivered, but you insisted on picking it up yourself."

"Yeah ok, but I picked it up from the loading area. I didn't come in that night," I recalled.

"Maybe you're right. Who knows? My days run together sometimes," Isis admitted.

We walked towards the massive bronze statue that appeared to be a replica of mine. "Speaking of that sculpture I found a camera in it," I revealed.

"That wasn't a camera. It was more like a projector, and the eyes would turn colors if you hit the small switch on the side. Different hues of green would brighten then dim continuously. It was that personal touch I spoke about earlier," she said sarcastically.

I sensed the sarcasm, but I casually ignored it. "I hate I didn't get a chance to even check it out. I just admired the piece aesthetically. I had no idea that it did anything."

"You see this one? I used different technology. I can push a button on this remote and the sky changes colors. There is even a rainbow option that I used during the shows. I have one that I'm working on. One that shows the elements: thunderstorms and things like that," Isis described.

"That's dope. I need you to make me another piece. I'm not sure of what, but my Atlas days are over. I will leave that for someone else while I enjoy the heavens without the condemnation of holding them up," I said.

We walked towards the back of the gallery in her personal space where the magic happened. She began putting a little switch in her hips like she knew I was watching.

"Let me show you this painting that I'm working on for Fast Money Forever. You know that's the record company that the Diamond King co-founded with Charles "Fast Money" Manuel. Anyway, they commissioned this painting and put a rush on it, so they can put the image on his posthumous album. Basically, they are going to remix the new album and add guest features as a tribute," she blurted out.

Even her nasally voice didn't bother me. It was as if she was seducing me with her work. I knew she was good, but to be surrounded by this level of talent must be like what an author feels like when writing their book in the middle of a library surrounded by inspiration.

"Yeah, that picture is going to be nice. But out of curiosity, why did you put him on a mattress with money on it?" I questioned.

"You know Fast Money said this was a picture worthy of his obituary. Here is the original," she said. She removed the picture taped to a wall next to her easel, and I'll be damn this muthafucka took pictures with my money and he was also fucking my bitch in my bed. I was boiling inside, but I didn't flinch.

"Yeah, that's an interesting picture. Do you know who the photographer was?" I pressed for more information.

"No, but I'm sure I can get the info and send it to you," Isis responded.

"Ok, baby. Thanks. I appreciate it. I have some other things to do, but I will be waiting on that info."

"Craft, if you could reconsider my offer, I would really appreciate you even more. I've been trying to call Dick, but it wasn't any answer. I have left messages, but I don't know."

"Yeah, I haven't been able to reach him either. I will give you the contact info of a friend of mines named Angie. She can be the person you can get in touch with if you can't reach me," I instructed.

"You replaced Dick?" she asked.

"Yeah, I got tired of him fucking around." We hugged probably longer than we should've and shorter than she would have liked. I grabbed a feel of her long buns before I left just for kicks, and she loved every bit of it. It was a nice firm squeeze with both hands. From the touch, I found out that she didn't have on any panties and her flat buns gotta little jiggle to them.

"Stop. It's been too long since I was last touched sexually. You're trying to start something and not finish it."

Damn, is that every woman's line that I run into, thinking to myself. I brushed off the thought and made my move towards the door, Isis followed briskly behind me. She kissed me on my cheek and her breath smelled of fresh mint and dark chocolate.

Chapter 22

The door closed as I made my way to Angie's direction. I returned to a world less intimate and more unforgiving. An older white lady strolled passed gripping her purse just by the sight of me. Her thin gold chain had three crosses on it, and I guess I was one of the thieves. "You're poorer than me," I said, walking with my head up. The mental games that those people play forces me to be well versed on how to combat them. Her fear and her ignorance won't define me nor dictate the way I operate or view myself.

My presence alone was threatening. The idea that I am more than just a nigga born to work, pay bills and die was threatening. Pawns pretending to be kings are always going to have a certain level of revulsion, because the life I live is the one that favors the bold. My smile through challenging times gives me strength in the face of enemies who wish I would be beheaded at the gallows and crucified in public. I tried to be a servant and kingly my whole life. Maybe it was a Messiah complex. I have found through my experiences that the Messiah is in fact a pawn to be used up and sacrificed when there is no longer any use.

Not all Messiahs receive martyrdom just like all pawns aren't remembered.

Stepping back into Angie's truck, I thought about how much I preferred to drive, but it hadn't been too bad having a driver. I need one for my new Phantom anyway.

"Why you looking like that?" Angie inquired.

"Like what?"

"Like somebody stole your dog," she painted with her words.

"No reason. I was just in deep thought about the world and the things around us," I responded still deep in thought.

"My friend at the police station finally got back to me. He said it was a male, probably white most likely from the bone structure. He said it was a pinky ring with the Star of David in diamonds," Angie explained.

"Damn, that sounds like Dick, but why would he be at my house in the first place? Is it too early to tell if he was dead already or died in the fire?"

"He didn't reveal the details, but he did say it was definitely a white dude," she said.

"Damn, slick Dick is up out of here; this shit is wild! Where is Stormy?" I said as I banged my hand in frustration on her dashboard.

"You break you buy," Angie joked in her best Chinese lady's voice.

"I wanted to talk to him first. At least look him in his eyes and see if he'd tell me the truth. He was saying I was running with the wrong crowd when his hypocritical ass had been running and stealing with the wrong muthafuckas!" I said angrily.

Angie began rubbing my back attempting to comfort me and calm me down. The knots in my neck disappeared with every methodical move. Hands like magic: soft but strong tricking the tension away.

"Have you ever thought of having some Craft men? You need some folks to do your heavy lifting for you," she instructed.

I turned my head towards her while she continued to remove the tension from my neck and back. "Craft men? I had that! Them niggas turned against me and your brother was one of them," I resisted.

"I'm not talking about opportunist you chilled with or made money with, but men and women dedicated to your vision and cause with no desire to rise to your height or your position. They trust your leadership and direction to the point where they will do the necessary deeds and never allow it to get back that you were involved or instructed certain actions," she explained thoroughly.

"You mean pawns?" I asked.

"No quit thinking of things like a game and people like chess pieces. Soldiers sound more noble than pawns."

"A soldier is a pawn," I assured her.

"Yeah, but which name will get the soldier to do more work."

"It depends on the soldier," I argued. Frustrated, she stopped rubbing my neck immediately and the knots seemed to come back instantly.

"Keep going. Don't stop that was feeling good, bae," I eagerly admitted.

"I will if you stop being a smart ass. Give them titles where they can presume to be more than what they are. Same responsibility, but a more respectable name. Call a stripper a dancer and a hooker an escort or call girl. The examples are endless," she insisted putting me up on game.

"So, this is what you've been thinking about while I was in there interrogating Isis?"

"I'm sure there was little interrogating going on. You probably was trying to fuck her. I know you," she blurted out.

"Girl, please. I ain't got time for that," I replied quickly.

"That lip gloss on your cheek suggest otherwise," Angie said, having an ah ha moment.

Isis was locking up for the day as we were discretely pulling off. "Hey Angie, pull over up there I want to see what car she gets in so we can follow her. She was talking some good shit, but that really looked like a camera and not a projector."

"What type shit you got going on? I'm surprised your freaky ass ain't got no cameras all through your house recording your many sexual deeds," she said, smiling.

"I didn't think I needed none of that shit, because the building has security and cameras already. Damn, that's it! We need to see who let Dick up into my building and if we can get the copies of them videos. Call your home boy and see if he can get us that info. That would help, especially since he already has insight on the situation anyway."

"So, are we following or calling?" she asked for clarity.

"Baby, we are doing both. Mash them buttons and that pedal!"

Chapter 23

A car arrived shortly to pick Isis up. A small red Toyota compact car. The driver seemed to have a dark complexion with straight hair appearing to be Indian or Middle Eastern, something along those lines. It was probably a driving service, but I still needed to eliminate her completely off the list of people who have bad intentions for me. Her face buried in her phone. The blue light reflected onto her dark colored lenses. Ear buds feed her mind the same substance that kept her intertwined with her surroundings. We let the car get ahead of us far enough that we couldn't be detected and close enough to keep an eye on our target.

"Slow it down, baby. We don't need to be that close," I cautioned.

"I hear you. I just don't want to lose them," she replied easing up on the gas a little.

"This ain't the movies. We don't need a car chase situation. We got them in eye range, and we are about two car lengths behind." The music was off, and we were following our prey at a controlled pace.

"Craft, I got my contact on the phone. He said he can meet us in an hour or two."

"Tell him two hours and to meet us at the hospital," I instructed her to relay. The darkening of the sky reminded me of the need to check on Ice. After about half an hour of stalking, we finally arrived in front of the King of Jokers Comedy Club. The place was packed, and the marquee glowed bright like the sun at night. Isis hopped out and headed to the express entrance of the building. The door person wearing all black with a red bowtie, greeted her with enthusiasm. He admired her curves and was aware of her angles.

"Hey Angie, you have to go inside on this one. I can't afford to be noticed, and she don't have a clue who you are."

"I don't have a clue who she is either," my partner in crime admitted.

"I will screen shot a picture of her and send it to you. Stop right here. I will circle the block for a parking spot," I said.

"What you want me to do when I find her?"

"Nothing. Just observe and see who she is with."

"One problem. How do I get in if she is V.I.P. and I don't even have a ticket?" she asked.

I pointed in the direction of the man with the red bowtie. "You see that person at the door who job title is probably a ticket technician?

However, they probably pay him like he's just a ticket collector," I replied being a smart ass.

"Yeah," she said while rolling her eyes.

I grabbed a few dollas' from my pocket, "Give him these 3 hundreds and you know the rest. Show me your honeypot skills."

"My what?" the double agent said in confusion.

"Never mind. Get through that door baby like I know you can. Put the hazards on. I'll watch you work. Fuck it if the people behind me start blowing their horns."

Chapter 24

Both of us exited the vehicle with our parts to play. I keenly observed from the driver's seat while Angie paid an underpaid employee to gain access to a venue that he probably couldn't afford to attend himself.

She successfully gained access using only a part of what I gave her, which is definitely a great move. I'm not going to mention it. I'm going to see if she does. If I can't trust her with a few hundred, then I won't test fate with several million. It's probably a crafty move on the part of my very first Craft men, but my radar has been a little off lately. It's the principle over the paper. As long as you have principles, you will always have the paper. People who put paper before principles tend to do anything if paper is presented first. Those folks are mercenaries, principles are for soldiers.

I can still smell the vodka on my father's breath. A wise man defeated by life, perhaps his principles should have included being more responsible with his paper. I started drinking vodka watching him intently as a child, his habits both good and bad. Momentarily drinking more to become closer to my father, unsuccessfully removed the wedge between us. No longer wanting to numb myself and drown in my sorrows, I healed and swam through the troubled waters under bridges I'd burned. His comfort zone was like the noose that tightened around his neck on the strong tree branch that was ready for him to eventually give up. He finally gave up and his lifeless body swung in the wind.

I circled the block and looked for somewhere to park. It didn't even have to be legit. I just needed to use it long enough while Double 0 yoga pants gathered the intelligence. A NO PARKING spot was posted, but "me no speak no English homes." Bored after sitting a few minutes, my mind drifted. I pealed scabs off wounds both physically and mentally as if I enjoyed watching myself bleed.

"Let's see what we have here," I checked the handle on her glove box, but it was locked. On the real, she ain't all the way past the background check. The compartment under her armrest looked like the junk drawer that everybody had in their kitchens in the neighborhood growing up. Sifting through that mess wasn't worth the time. Finally, Angie texted me. "About damn time," I said to myself.

9:15 p.m.

Angie: I see her, but she looks like she is by
herself. I only used $100.00
and my feminine wilds. That nigga was
thirsty. The other two hundred will be
for research: you know drinks, food, and
maybe even a souvenir T-Shirt.

9:16 p.m.

Me: Cool, I ain't mad atcha. If we can save
money together, then we can make
money together.

9:16 p.m.

Angie: :) :) :)

Chapter 25

Sneaking in will be better than sittin' out here having my mind wondering about my pops, Church, Ice and all of the rest of the shit I got going on, I thought. I tried to convince myself while time stood still. Checking my phone, his wife didn't even return my calls or let me know if she was in town to claim the body. Hell, I don't even know if they know where his body is. His head was missing and it didn't even make the news. You would think it was conspiracy, but it's common practice in the media.

My feelings were mixed about Dick's crooked ass. I must find out if he was dead or alive when my place went ablaze. He played a part in my missing money from the trusts as well as the dock situation that got me implicated and almost killed. Tricky Dick had been real busy being the pot calling the kettle black. Tags was out here trying to take over the world brick by brick.

"Can't wait to see that muthafucka cause it's on sight, "I paused the thoughts in my head speaking out loud.

He weaved a web so wicked that if I wasn't one of the intended victims, I would shake his hand on strategy and execution, respectively. But "greed will always rule the cheese." I quoted my pops a lot lately. I wondered if that was a sign of some kind. If he wasn't so greedy and didn't offend that Mexican cartel, then the murder squad wouldn't be hunting his ass. Which became a hidden blessing for me. It was the action that got me to react and think about things beyond the chessboard, but even more universally. Not like a jack-of-all-trades. I was a student of the game knowing the intricate ways how many games were not only played but won.

"There go an empty spot right there." It might be kinda tight, but I'mma whip it in. BEEP! BEEP! "Hold up." Damn people be acting impatient. The parking spot was secured after two tries, but I was in it to win it. I had to give Mr. Bowtie a try at the door. He was about my height, but on the huskier end. He was about 10 plus years younger, and the only time he got some was if he was paying for it. Facts. He looked like his breath stank.

My approach was discreet on some player shit. He wasn't having it. That nigga played defense, and I was the one trying to get the little hating nigga paid in the first place.

"I forgot my ticket. I just need to get my wife, so we can leave." I lied quickly.

"Sorry, sir. No ticket, no entry. I can't afford to lose my job trying to give you the hook up," the doorman said, voice trembling.

"I don't need a hook up. I need to grab my wife, so we can go. We had a family emergency," I added.

"Sir, I'm going to have to ask you to leave. If you refuse, I'll have to call security to remove you."

"Remove me! Call 'em then muthafucka! I'mma be right here and tell them the same thing that I told you. You must don't know who I am. I'mma have your ass fired in the a.m.," I warned. Those words hit hard like I intended. People in the nearby line were starting to look at us, and pulling out phones just in case it was going to be a World Star moment.

"I usually don't do this, sir. It's against company policy, but I will let you in this one time," his voice shaky, but he was more embarrassed by the attention then the fact that I didn't fear his threats, recognize his authority, or lack thereof.

"Thank you, young man. One time is all I need." I offered him money from the beginning, but he refused. It was like he was a man of principle. In all actuality though, he was a mercenary pretending. It was a nice crowd. Not everyone was seated yet, so they were doing an open mic to warm up the crowd. The amateur comics and amateur sleuths made their debuts on the same night at the same time. That must be a good omen.

9:48 p.m.
Me: Where you at?

I texted Angie while making my way through the crowd that seemed to be bunched in certain spots trying to get to their tables or booths. Champagne on ice and reserved signs were on the tables. People spent a little something to enjoy this night. Me and Stormy would do it big like that, but Ice was the total opposite like she wanted me to know that she wasn't after my money. Stormy has her own money, so I never even thought she would ever steal some money from me. But hey, you live, and you learn. There were a couple of laughs here and there, but it seemed like that fella was going to have to work on his material, or let someone else do the jokes. The couples looked nice together: color coordinated with the commercial look of love on their faces. They looked how people say you're supposed to look even if it is only for one night. A couple who wasn't smiling hard and pulling out chairs may be perceived as unhappy; when in fact, they have their relationships down to the point where they can grow and accomplish things together versus being together for a long period of time with little to no growth to show. Just the commercialized smile that people copy from T.V.

Comedy is something I always enjoyed, but it ain't for me. I'm a shower comic or a bedroom comic. That stage was too revealing, too personal, even beyond the scope of my poetry and podcast. My words are true without validation. A comic must have validation nightly getting the approval of strangers who may or may not find his method of truth amusing. One thing about comedy, it's a vehicle where you can talk about many serious subjects light-heartedly.

Religion, politics, relationships, race and whatever else was relevant.

10:06 p.m.
Angie: I'm working. She is still sitting
　　　　by herself. I'm thinking about going
　　　　over there and talking to her just to see
　　　　if I can get a seat. My feet tired. I would
　　　　have worn different shoes if I knew I

was doing more than a stakeout from the car.

10:07 p.m.

Me: Don't take your ass over there and mess things up! You probably somewhere posted watching the comedy show instead of watching Isis.

10:09 p.m.

Angie: SMH yeah. I did peep the last guy for a second. That roach joke was funny. He just cussed too much with his roach lookin' ass.

I didn't even text back. I got to keep an eye on Isis myself. The sooner I find her, the better. My wardrobe fitin' well: something sporty and casual with some nice driver loafers. I just needed to stay below the ...... "Craft what are you doing here?" I didn't even have to turn around. I knew by the nasally voice that it was Isis.

"Twice in one day? What a coincidence. I'm here looking for a friend. What are you doing here?" I responded.

"I come here often, so I can unwind. I think about going on stage just to try my hand at comedy, but I'm comfortable learning from my booth," she said, pointing in the direction of her reserved booth. The champagne was still in the bucket unopened.

"You here all by yourself?" I shouted over the laughter.

"Yeah. I was until you came. You are more than welcome to join me, at least until you find your friend," she offered.

"I can't. It's tempting, definitely," I nodded while responding.

"I insist," she replied grabbing my arm firmly and leading me to her private booth in the center of the place 50 feet from center stage.

Unaware that Angie called me, because my ringer was drowned out by laughter, after the second attempt, she texted me.

10:15 p.m.

Angie: Oh, hell naw! What you doing in here
            all hugged up and shit? I hope yawl got
            room, cause' I'm on my way.

www.ingramcontent.com/pod-product-compliance
Lightning Source LLC
Chambersburg PA
CBHW071007280626
47160CB00015B/1930